Damon and Delia

William Godwin

Contents

DAMON AND DELIA

BY

William Godwin

PART the FIRST.

CHAPTER I.

Containing introductory matter.

The races at Southampton have, for time immemorial, constituted a scene of rivalship, war, and envy. All the passions incident to the human frame have here assumed as true a scope, as in the more noisy and more tragical contentions of statesmen and warriors. Here nature has displayed her most hidden attractions, and art has furnished out the artillery of beauty. Here the coquet has surprised, and the love-sick nymph has sapped the heart of the unwary swain. The scene has been equally sought by the bolder and more haughty, as by the timid sex. Here the foxhunter has sought a new subject of his boast in the ***nonchalance*** of ***dishabille***; the peer has played off the dazzling charms of a coronet and a star; and the ***petit maitre*** has employed the anxious niceties of dress.

Of all the beauties in this brilliant circle, she, who was incomparably the most celebrated, was the graceful Delia. Her person, though not absolutely tall, had an air of dignity. Her form was bewitching, and her neck was alabaster. Her cheeks glowed with the lovely vermilion of nature, her mouth was small and pouting, her lips were coral, and her teeth whiter than the driven snow. Her forehead was bold, high, and polished, her eyebrows were arched, and from beneath them her fine blue eyes shone with intelligence, and sparkled with heedless gaiety. Her hair was of the brightest auburn, it was in the greatest abundance, and when, unfettered by the ligaments of fashion, it flowed about her shoulders and her lovely neck, it presented the most ravishing object that can possibly be imagined.

With all this beauty, it Cannot be supposed but that Delia was followed by a train of admirers. The celebrated Mr. Prattle, for whom a thousand fair ones cracked their fans and tore their caps, was one of the first to enlist himself among her ador- ers. Squire Savage, the fox-hunter, who, like Hippolitus of old, chased the wily fox and timid hare, and had never yet acknowledged the empire of beauty, was subdued by the artless sweetness of Delia. Nay, it has been reported, that the incomparable lord Martin, a peer of ten thousand pounds a year, had made advances to her father. It is true, his lordship was scarcely four feet three inches in stature, his belly was prominent, one leg was half a foot shorter, and one shoulder half a foot higher than the other. His temper was as crooked as his shape; the sight of a happy human being would give him the spleen; and no mortal man could long reside under the same roof with him. But in spite of these trifling imperfections, it has been confidently affirmed, that some of the haughtiest beauties of Hampshire would have been proud of his alliance.

Thus assailed with all the temptations that human nature could furnish, it might naturally be supposed, that Delia had long since resigned her heart. But in this conjecture, however natural, the reader will find himself mistaken. She seemed as coy as Daphne, and as cold as Diana. She diverted herself indeed with the insig- nificant loquaciousness of Mr. Prattle, and the aukward gallantry of the Squire; but she never bestowed upon either a serious thought. And for lord Martin, who was indisputably allowed to be the best match in the county, she could not bear to hear him named with patience, and she always turned pale at the sight of him.

But Delia was not destined always to laugh at the darts of Cupid. Mrs. Bridget her waiting maid, delighted to run over the list of her adorers, and she was much more eloquent and more copious upon the subject than we have been. When her mistress received the mention of each with gay indifference, Mrs. Bridget would close the dialogue, and with a sagacious look, and a shake of her head, would tell the lovely Delia, that the longer it was before her time came, the more surely and the more deeply she would be caught at last. And to say truth, the wisest philosopher might have joined in the verdict of the sage Bridget. There was a softness in the temper of Delia, that seemed particularly formed for the tender passion. The voice of misery never assailed her ear in vain. Her purse was always open to the orphan, the maimed, and the sick. After reading a tender tale of love, the intricacies of the Princess of Cleves, the soft distress of Sophia Western, or the more modern story of the Sorrows of Werter, her gentle breast would heave with sighs, and her eye, suffused with tears, confess a congenial spirit.

The father of Delia--let the reader drop a tear over this blot in our little narrative--had once been a tradesman. He was naturally phlegmatic, methodical, and avaricious. His ear was formed to relish better the hoarse voice of an exchange broker, than the finest tones of Handel's organ. He found something much more agreeable and interesting in the perusal of his ledger and his day book, than in the scenes of Shakespeare, or the elegance of Addison. With this disposition, he had notwithstanding, when age had chilled the vigour of his limbs, and scattered her snow over those hairs which had escaped the hands of the barber, resigned his shop, and retired to enjoy the fruits of his industry. It is as natural for a tradesman in modern times to desire to die in the tranquillity of a gentleman, as it was for the Saxon kings of the Heptarchy to act the same inevitable scene amidst the severities of a cloister.

The old gentleman however found, and it is not impossible that some of his brethren may have found it before him, when the great transaction was irretrievably over, that retirement and indolence did not constitute the situation for which either nature or habit had fitted him. It has been observed by some of those philosophers who have made the human mind the object of their study, that idleness is often the mother of love. It might indeed have been supposed, that Mr. Hartley, for that was his name, by having attained the age of sixty, might have outlived every danger of this kind. But opportunity and temptation supplied that, which might have been deficient on the side of nature.

Within a little mile of the mansion in which he had taken up his retreat, resided two ancient maiden ladies. Under cover of the venerable age to which they had attained, they had laid aside many of those modes which coyness and modesty have prescribed to their sex. The visits of a man were avowedly as welcome to them, and indeed much more so, than those of a woman. Their want of attractions either external or mental, had indeed hindered the circle of their acquaintance from being very extensive; but there were some, as well as Mr. Hartley, who preferred the company of ugliness, censoriousness and ill nature to solitude.

Such were the Miss Cranley's, the name of the elder of whom was Amelia, and that of the younger Sophia. Miss Amelia was nominally forty, and her sister thirty years of age. Perhaps if we stated the matter more accurately, we should rate the elder at fifty-six, and the younger somewhere about fifty. They both of them were masculine in their behaviour, and studious in their disposition. Miss Amelia, delighted in the study of theology; she disputed with the curate, maintained a godly correspondence with a neighbouring cobler, and was even said to be preparing a pamphlet in defence of the dogmas of Mr. Whitfield. Miss Sophia, who will make a much more considerable figure in this history, was altogether as indefatigable in the study of politics, as her sister was in that of theology. She adhered indeed to none of our political parties, for she suspected and despised them all. My lord North she treated as stupid, sleepy, and void of personal principle. Mr. Fox was a brawling gamester, devoid of all attachments but that of ambition, and who treated the mob with flattery and contempt. Mr. Burke was a Jesuit in disguise, who under the most specious professions, was capable of the blackest and meanest actions. For her own part she was a steady republican. That couplet of Dr. Garth was continually in her mouth,

> From my very soul I hate,
> All kings and ministers of state.

CHAPTER II.
A Ball.

Thus much it was necessary to premise, in order to acquaint the reader with the situation of our heroine, and that of some other personages in this history. Having discharged this task, we will return to the point from which we set out.

It was at one of the balls at the races at Southampton--the company was already assembled. The card tables were set, and our maiden ladies, together with many other venerable pieces of antiquity, were assembled around them. In another and more spacious room, appeared all that Southampton could boast of youth and beauty. The squire and his sister, Mr. Prattle, and lord Martin, formed a part of the company. The first bustle was nearly composed, when Damon entered the assembly.

He appeared to be a stranger to every body present. And, as he is equally a stranger to our readers, we will now announce him in proper form. Damon appeared to be about twenty years of age. His person was tall, and his limbs slender and well formed. His dress was elegance itself. His coat was ornamented with a profusion of lace, and the diamond sparkled in his shoe. His countenance was manly and erect. There appeared in it a noble confidence, which the spectator would at first sight ascribe to dignity of birth, and a perfect familiarity with whatever is elegant and polite. This confidence however had not the least alloy of *hauteur*, his eye expressed the most open sensibility and the kindest sympathy.

There is something undescribably interesting in the figure we have delineated. The moment our hero entered the room, the attention of every person present was fixed upon him. The master of the ceremonies immediately advanced, and escorted him to the most honourable seat that yet remained vacant. While Damon examined with an eager eye the gay parterre of beauty that appeared before him, a general whisper was excited upon his account. "Who is he?" "Who is he?" echoed from every corner of the room. But while curiosity was busy in his enquiries, there was not an individual capable of satisfying them.

The business of every one was now the choice of a partner. But as one object had engrossed the attention of all, they were willing to see the election he would make, though every one feared to lose the partner he had destined for himself. Damon was therefore, however unwilling to distinguish himself in so particular a manner, constrained to advance the foremost. He passed slightly along before a considerable number, who sat in expectation. At length he approached the seat of Delia. He bowed to her in the most graceful manner, and intreated to be honoured with her hand. She smiled assent, and they crossed the room among a croud of envious rivals. Besides the lovers we had mentioned, there were four others, who had secretly determined to dance with Delia.

But if the gentlemen were disappointed, to whose eyes the beauty of Delia, however unrivalled, was familiar, the disappointment and envy of the fair sex upon the loss of Damon, whose external and natural recommendations had beside the grace of novelty, were inexpressible. The daughter of Mr. Griskin, an eminent butcher in Clare-market, who had indeed from nature, the grace of being cross-eyed, now looked in ten thousand more various directions than she ever did before. Miss Prim, agitated in every limb, cracked her fan into twenty pieces. Miss Gawky, who had unfortunately been initiated by the chamber maid in the art of snuff-taking, plied her box with more zeal than ever. Miss Languish actually fainted, and was with some difficulty conveyed into the air. Such was the confusion occasioned in the ball at Southampton, by the election of Damon.

Affairs being now somewhat adjusted, the dances began. Damon at every interval addressed himself to his lovely partner in the easiest and most elegant conversation. He talked with fluency, and his air and manner gave a grace and dignity to the most trifling topics. The heart of Delia, acknowledged the charms of youthful beauty and graceful deportment, and secretly confessed that it had never before encountered so formidable an enemy.

When the usual topics of conversation had been exhausted, the behaviour of Damon became insensibly more particular, he pressed her hand with the most melting ardour, and a sigh ever and anon escaped from his breast. He paid her several very elegant compliments, though they were all of them confined within the limits of decorum. Delia, on the other hand, though she apparently received them with the most gay indifference, in reality drank deep of the poison of love, and the words of Damon made an impression upon her heart, that was not easily to be erased.

But however delicious was the scene in which they were engaged, it necessarily drew to a conclusion. The drowsy clocks now announced the hour of three in the morning. The dances broke up, and the company separated. Delia leaped into the chariot that was waiting, and quickly arrived at the parental mansion. Fatigued with the various objects that had passed before her, she immediately retired to rest. For some time however a busy train of thoughts detained her from the empire of sleep. "How lovely a stranger! How elegant his manners, and how brilliant his wit! How soft and engaging the whole of his behaviour! But ah! was this the fruit of reverence and admiration? Might it not be no more than general gallantry? Oh that I were mistress of his heart! That he would lay his person at my feet! What a contrast between him and my former admirers! How doubly hateful does lord Martin, the lover favoured by my father now appear! But ah! who is this Damon? What is his fortune, and what his pretensions? His dress surely bespoke him a man of rank. His elegant manners could have been learned in no vulgar circle. How sweet, methinks is suspence! How delightful the uncertainty that hangs about him! And yet, how glad should I be to have my doubts resolved."

Soothed with these and similar reflections, the lovely maid fell asleep. But even in sleep she did not forget the impressions she had received. She imagined that Damon now approached her pillow. But how unlike the Damon she had seen! His eyes had something in them superior to a mortal. His shoulders were adorned with wings, and a vest of celestial azure flowed around him. He smiled upon her with the most bewitching grace. But the gentle maid involuntarily stretched out her arms towards him, and the pleasing vision vanished from her sight.

Again she closed her eyes, and again she endeavoured to regain her former object. Damon indeed appeared, but in how different a manner! his countenance was impressed with every mark of horror, and he seemed to fly before some who inveterately pursued him. They appeared with the countenances of furies, and the snakes hissed around their temples. Delia looked earnestly upon them, and presently recollected the features of the admirers we have already celebrated. The noble peer under the figure of Tisiphone, led the troop. Damon stumbled and fell. Sudden as lightning Tisiphone reached the spot, and plunged a dagger in his heart. She drew it forth reeking with blood, and the lovely youth appeared in the agonies of death. Terrified beyond measure, Delia screamed with horror and awoke.

In the midst of reveries like these, now agitated with apprehension, and now soothed with pleasure, Delia passed the night. The sun appeared, her gold repeater informed her that it was twelve, and, assisted by the fair hands of Mrs. Bridget, she began to rise.

CHAPTER III.
A Ghost.

Mr. Hartley had breakfasted and walked out in the fields, before Delia appeared. She had scarcely begun her morning repast, ere Miss Fletcher, the favourite companion and confidante of Delia, entered the room. "My dearest creature," cried the visitor, "how do you do? Had not we not a most charming evening? I vow I was fatigued to death: and then, lord Martin, I think he never appeared to so much advantage. Why he was quite covered with diamonds, spangles, and frogs." "Ah!" cried Delia, "but the young stranger." "True," answered Miss Fletcher, "I liked him of all things; so tall, so genteel, and so sweetly perfumed.--I cannot think who he is. I called upon Miss Griskin, and I called upon Miss Savage, nobody knows. He is some great man." "When did he come to town?" said Delia, "Where does he lodge?" "My dear, he came to town yesterday in the evening, and went away again as soon as the ball was over. But do not you think that Mr. Prattle's new suit of scarlet sattin was vastly becoming? I vow I could have fallen in love with him. He is so gay and so trifling, and so fond of hearing himself talk. Why, does not he say a number of smart things?" "It is exessively strange," said Delia. (She was thinking of the stranger.) But Miss Fletcher went on--"Not at all, my life. Upon my word I think he is always very entertaining. He cuts out paper so prettily, and he has drawn me the sweetest pattern for an apron. I vow, I think, I never showed you it." "What can be his name?" said Delia; "His name, my dear; law, child, you do not hear a word one says to you. But of all things, give me the green coat and pink breeches of Mr. Savage. But did you ever hear the like? There will be a terrible to do--Lord Martin is in such a quandary--He has sent people far and near." "I wish they may find him," exclaimed Delia. "Nay, if they do, I would not be in his shoes for the world. My lord vows revenge. He says he is his rival. Why, child, the stranger did not make love to you, did he?" "Mercy on us," cried Delia, "then my dream is out." "Oh, bless us," said Miss Fletcher, "what dream, my dear?" Her curiosity then prevailed upon her to be silent for a few moments, while Delia related that with which the reader is already acquainted.

In return, Delia requested of her friend to explain to her more intelligibly what she hinted of the anger of lord Martin. "Why, my dear, his lordship has been employed all this morning in writing challenges. They say he has not writ less than a dozen, and has sent them by as many messengers, like a hue and cry, all over the county--my lord is a little man--but what of that--he is as stout as Hercules, and as brave as what-d'ye call'um, that you and I read of in Pope's Homer. He is in such a vengeance of a passion, that he cannot contain himself. He tells it to every body he sees; and his mother and sister run about the house screaming and fainting like so many mad things."

Delia, as we have already said, was endowed with a competent share of natural understanding. She therefore easily perceived, that from an anger so boisterous and so public, no very fatal effects were to be apprehended. This reflection quieted the terrors that her dream had excited, and which the young partiality she began to feel for the amiable stranger would otherwise have confirmed. Her breast being thus calmed, she made about half a dozen morning visits, among which, one to Miss Griskin, and another to Miss Languish, were included. The conversation every where turned upon the outrageousness of lord Martin. All but the gentle Delia, were full of anxiety and expectation. The females were broken into parties respecting the event of the duel. Many trembled for the fate of lord Martin, so splendid, so rich, and consequently, in their opinion, so amiable and so witty. Others, guided by the unadulterated sentiments of nature, poured forth all their vows for the courteous unknown. "May those active limbs remain without a wound! May his elegant blue and silver never be stained with blood! Ah, what a pity, that eyes so bright, and teeth so white, should be shrowded in the darkness of the grave."

The dinner, a vulgar meal, that passed exactly in the same manner as fifty dinners had before it, shall be consigned to silence. The evening was bright and calm. It was in the close of autumn; and every thing tempted our lovely fair one to take the air. By the way she called upon her inseparable friend and companion. They directed their course towards the sea side.

Here they had not advanced far, before they entered a grove, a spot particularly the favourite of Delia. In a little opening there was a bank embroidered with daisies and butter-cups; a little row of willows bending their heads forward, formed a kind of canopy; and directly before it, there was a vista through the trees, which afforded a distant prospect of the sea, with every here and there a vessel passing along, and the beams of the setting sun quivered on the waves.

Delia and her companion advanced towards the well known spot. The mellow voice of the thrush, and the clear pipe of the blackbird, diversified at intervals with the tender notes of the nightingale, formed the most agreable natural concert. The breast of Delia, framed for softness and melancholy, was filled with sensations responsive to the objects around her, and even the eternal clack of Miss Fletcher was still.

Presently, however, a new and unexpected object claimed their attention. A note, stronger and sweeter than that of any of the native choristers of the grove, swelled upon the air, and floated towards them. Having approached a few paces, they stood still to listen. It seemed to proceed from a flute, played upon by a human voice. The air was melancholy, but the skill was divine.

The native curiosity of Miss Fletcher was not upon this occasion a match for the sympathetic spirit of Delia. She pressed forward with an eager and uncertain step, and looking through an interstice formed by two venerable oaks, she perceived the figure of a young man sitting in her favourite alcove. His back was turned towards the side upon which she was. Having finished the air, he threw his flute carelessly from him, and folded his arms in a posture the most disconsolate that can be imagined. He rose and advanced a little with an irregular step. "Ah lovely mistress of my soul," cried he, "thou little regardest the anguish that must for ever be an inmate of this breast! While I am a prey to a thousand tormenting imaginations, thou riotest in the empire of beauty, heedless of the wounds thou inflicted, and the slaves thou chainest to thy chariot. Wretch that I am, what is to be done? But I must think no more." Saying this he snatched up his flute, and thrusting it into his bosom, hurried out of the grove.

While he spoke, Delia imagined that the voice was one that she had heard before though she knew not where. Her heart whispered her something more than her understanding could disentangle. But as he stooped to take his flute from the ground his profile was necessarily turned towards the inner part of the grove. Delia started and trembled. Damon stood confessed. But she scarcely recollected his features before he rushed away swifter than the winged hawk, and was immediately out of sight.

Delia was too full of a thousand reflections upon this unexpected rencounter to be able to utter a word. But Miss Fletcher immediately began. "God bless us," cried she, "did you ever see the like? Why it is my belief it is a ghost or a wizard. I never heard any thing so pretty--I vow, I am terribly frightened."

Delia now caught hold of her arm. "For heaven's sake, let us quit the grove. I do not know what is the matter--but I feel myself quite sick." "Good God! good heavens! Well, I do not wonder you are all in a tremble--But suppose now it should be nothing but Mr. Prattle--He is always somewhere or other--And then he plays *God save the king*, and *Darby and Joan*, like any thing." "Oh," said the lovely, trembling nymph, "they were the sweetest notes!" "Ah," said her companion, "he is a fine man. And then he is so modest--He will play at one and thirty, and ride upon a stick with little Tommy all day long. But sure it could not be Mr. Prattle--He always wears his hair in a queue you know--but the ghost had a bag and solitaire." "Well," cried Delia, "let us think no more of it. But did we hear anything?"--"Law, child, why he played the nicest glee--and then he made such a speech, for all the world like Mr. Button, that I like so to see in Hamlet." "True," said Delia,--"but what he said was more like the soft complainings of my dear Castalio. Did not he complain of a false mistress?" "Why he did say something of that kind.--If it be neither a ghost nor Mr. Prattle. I hope in God he is going to appear upon the Southampton stage. I do so love to see a fine young man come on for the first time with

> *May this alspishus day be ever sacred!* Or,
> *I am thy father's spirit."*

CHAPTER IV.
A Love Scene.

In such conversation the moments passed till they reached the habitation of Mr. Hartley. Miss Fletcher now took her leave. And after a supper as dull, and much more tedious to Delia, than the dinner, she retired to her chamber.

She retired indeed, but not to rest. Her brain was filled with a croud of uneasy thoughts. "Alas," said she, "how short has been the illusion!--But yesterday, I was flushed with all the pride of conquest, and busily framed a thousand schemes of ideal happiness--Where are they now?--The lovely youth, the only man I ever saw in whose favour my heart was prepossessed, and with whom I should have felt no repugnance to have engaged in the tenderest ties, is nothing to me--He loves another. He too complains of slighted passion, and ill-fated love. Ah, had he made his happiness depend on me, what would not I have done to reward him! Carefully I would have soothed every anguish, and taught his heart to bound with joy. But what am I saying?--Where am I going?--Am I that Delia that bad defiance to the art of men,--that saw with indifference the havock that my charms had made! With every opening morn I smiled. Each hour was sped with joy, and my heart was light and frolic. And shall I dwindle into a pensive, melancholy maid, the sacrifice of one that heeds me not, whose sighs no answering sighs encounter!--let it not be said. I have hitherto asserted the independence of my sex, I will continue to do so. Too amiable unknown, I give thee to the winds! Propitious fate, I thank thee that thou hast so soon discovered how much my partiality was misplaced. I will abjure it before it be too late. I will tear the little intruder from my heart before the mischief is become irretrievable."

The following evening Delia repaired again by a kind of irresistible impulse to the grove. She asked not the company of her friend. She dared alone hazard the encounter of that object, at which she had trembled so much the preceding day. Unknown to herself she still imaged a kind of uncertainty in her fate which would not permit her to lay aside all thought of Damon. She determined at all events, to have her doubts resolved. "When there is no longer," said she to herself, "any room for mistake, I shall then know what to do."

As she drew near the alcove, she perceived the same figure stretched along the bank, and with his eyes immoveably fixed upon a little fountain that rose in a corner of the scene. He seemed lost in thought. Delia approached doubtfully, but he heard her not. Advanced near to her object, she reclined forward in a posture of wonder and attention. At this moment a sigh burst from the heart of Damon, and he raised himself upon the seat.

His eyes caught the figure of Delia.------"Ah," said he, starting from his trance, "what do I see? Art thou, lovely intruder, a mere vision, an aerial being that shuns the touch?" "I beg ten thousand pardons. I meaned not, sir, to interrupt you. I will be gone." "No, go not." Answered he. "Thou art welcome to my troubled thoughts. I could gaze for ever."

Saying this he rose and advancing towards her, seized her hand. "Be not afraid," said he, "gentle fair one, my breast is a stranger to violence and rudeness. I have felt the dart of love. Unhappy myself, I learn to feel for others. But you are happy." As he said this, a tear unbidden stole into the eye of Delia, and she wiped it away with the hand which was disengaged from his. "And dost thou pity me," said he. "And does such softness dwell within thy breast? If you knew the story of my woes, you would have reason to pity me. I am in love to destraction, but I dare not disclose my passion. I am banished from the presence of her I love. Ah, cruel fate, I am entangled, inextricably entangled." "And how, sir," said Delia, "can I serve you?" "Alas," said he, in no way. My case is hopeless and irretrievable. And what am I doing? Why do I talk, when the season calls for action? Oh, I am lost."

"Dear Sir," answered Delia, "you terrify me to death." "Oh, no. I would not for the world give you an uneasy moment. Let me be unhappy--but may misfortune never disturb your tranquility. I return to seek her whose fate is surely destined to mix with mine. Pardon, loveliest of thy sex, the distraction in which I have appeared. I would ask you to forget me--I would ask you to remember me--I know not what I am, or what to think."

With these words he took the hand which he still held in one of his, and raising it to his lips, kissed it with the utmost fervour. Immediately he caught up his hat, which lay beside him on the ground, and began to advance along the path that led out of the grove on the side furthest from the town. But his eyes were still fixed upon Delia. He heeded not the path by which he went; and scarcely had he gone twenty paces, ere he changed his mind and returned. Delia was seated on the bank and seemed lost in reverie. Damon threw himself upon his knees before her.

"Ah, why," said he, "am I constrained to depart!--Why must I talk in riddles! Perhaps we may never see each other more. Perhaps the time will come when I shall be able to clear up the obscurity that at present I am obliged to preserve. But no, it cannot be. I never was happy but for two poor hours that I enjoyed your smiles, and, drinking in the poison of your charms, I forgot myself. The time too soon arrived for bitter recollection. My mistress calls, the mistress of my fate. I must be gone--Farewel--for ever."

Saying this, he heaved a sigh that seemed almost to tear his breast asunder, and with the utmost apparent violence he tore himself away, and rushed along the path with incredible velocity.

Delia was now alone. But instead, as she had flattered herself of having her doubts resolved, she was more uncertain, more perplexed than ever. "What" cried she, "can all this mean? How strange, and how inexplicable! Is it a real person that I have seen, or is it a vision that mocks my fancy? Am I loved, or am I hated? Oh, foolish question! Oh, fond illusion! Are we not parted for ever! Is he not gone to seek the mistress of his soul! Alas, he views me not, but with that general complacency, which youth, and the small pretensions I have to beauty are calculated to excite! He had nothing to relate that concerned myself, he merely intended to make me the confidante of his passion for another. Too surely he is unhappy. His heart seemed ready to burst with sorrow. Probably in this situation there is no greater or more immediate relief, than to disclose the subject of our distress, and to receive into our bosom the sympathetic tear of a simple and a generous heart. His behaviour today corresponds but too well with the suspicions that yesterday excited. Oh, Delia! then," added she, "be firm. Thou shalt see the conqueror no more. Think of him no more."

In spite however of all the resolution she could muster, Delia repaired day after day, sometimes alone, and sometimes in company with her friend, to that spot which, by the umbrage of melancholy it wore, was become more interesting than ever. Miss Fletcher, could scarcely at first be persuaded to direct her course that way, lest she should again see the ghost. But she need not have terrified herself. No ghost appeared.

Disappointed and baffled on this side, Delia by the strictest enquiries endeavoured to find out who the unknown person was, in whose fate she had become so greatly interested. The result of these enquiries, however diligent, was not entirely satisfactory. She learned that he had been for a few days upon a visit to a Mr. Moreland, a gentleman who lived about three miles from Southampton.

Mr. Moreland was a person of a very singular character. He had the reputation in the neighbourhood of being a cynic, a misanthrope, and a madman. He kept very little company, and was even seldom seen but by night. He had a garden sufficiently spacious, which was carefully rendered impervious to every human eye. And to this and his house he entirely confined himself in the day-time. The persons he saw were not the gentlemen of the neighbourhood. He had no toleration for characters that did not interest him. When he first came down to his present residence, he was visited by Mr. Hartley, Mr. Prattle, squire Savage, lord Martin, and all the most admired personages in the country. But their visits had never been returned. Mr. Prattle pronounced him a scoundrel; squire Savage said he was a nincompoop; and lord Martin was near sending him a challenge. But the censures of the former, and the threats of the latter, had never reached his ears. His domestics were numerous, but they were hired from a distance, and were permitted as little communication as possible with the powdered lacquies of Southampton. Of consequence, however much the unaccommodating conduct of Mr. Moreland disposed his neighbours to calumniate him, scandal was deprived of that daily food which is requisite for her subsistence, and the name of that gentleman was scarcely ever heard.

CHAPTER V.
A Man of Humour.

We will now return to lord Martin. All his messengers, from what cruel fate we cannot exactly ascertain, miscarried; and it was not till Damon had left the country, that he learned that he had been a visitor at the house of Mr. Moreland. Finding that he had missed his expected vengeance, he discharged his anger in unavailing curses, and for three days he breathed nothing but daggers, death, and damnation. Having thus vapoured away the paroxysm of his fury, he became tolerably composed.

But adverse fate had decreed a short duration to the tranquility of his lordship. Scarcely had the field been cleared from the enemy he so greatly dreaded, ere a new rival came upon the stage, to whose arms, though without any great foundation, the whole town of Southampton had consigned the charming Delia.

The name of this gentleman was Prettyman. He was just returned from his travels, and was reckoned perfectly accomplished. He was six foot high, his shoulders were broad, his legs brawny, and his whole person athletic. The habits however he had formed to himself in foreign countries, will not perhaps be allowed exactly to correspond with the figure which nature had bestowed upon him. He generally spent two hours every morning at his toilette. His face was painted and patched, his whole person strongly perfumed, and he had continually in his hand a gold snuff-box set with diamonds. His voice was naturally hoarse and loud, but with infinite industry he had brought himself to a pronunciation shrill, piping, and effeminate. His conversion was larded with foreign phrases and foreign oaths, and every thing he said was accompanied with a significant shrug.

The same period which had introduced this new pretender to the heart of Delia, had been distinguished by the arrival of a Sir William Twyford, who paid his addresses to Miss Fletcher. Sir William was exactly the reverse of Mr. Prettyman. With a genteel person, and an open and agreable phisiognomy, his manners were perfectly careless and unstudied. A predominant feature in his character was good nature. But this was not his ruling passion. He had an infinite fund of wit and humour, and he never was so happy as when he was able to place the foibles of affectation in a whimsical and ridiculous light.

As it was vanity alone, that had induced Mr. Prettyman to pay his addresses to the lady, who was universally allowed to surpass in beauty and every elegant accomplishment in the place in which he was, he would have been less pleased that his amour should have terminated in a marriage, than that by his affectation and coquetry he might break the heart of the simple fair one. Accordingly, it was his business to make the affair as public as possible.

Lord Martin, had been sufficiently irritated by the pretensions of Damon. The new intruder had wrought up his passion to the highest pitch. In the mean time he had renewed an acquaintance which he had formerly made with sir William Twyford. Sir William, upon all occasions, cultivated the intimacy of such, as, by any striking peculiarities, seemed to furnish a proper subject for his humour. He now contributed every thing in his power to inflame his lordship against Mr. Prettyman. He offered to become the bearer of a challenge, and to be his lordship's second in any future combat.

Lord Martin broke off the conversation somewhat abruptly, and began to reflect with himself upon what had passed. He had hitherto contrived, by some means or other, though he dealt very largely in challenges, never to have come to actual battle. But he had too much reason to think, that if he made sir William his messenger, he should not be able with any degree of honour to contrive an evasion. "It is true," said he, "I am in a most confounded passion, but a wise general never proceeds to action without having first deliberated. Zounds, blood and fire! would I could put an end to the existence of so presumptuous a villain! But then it must be considered that Mr. Prettyman is six foot high, and I am not five. He is as athletic as Ajax, but to me nature has been unfavourable. It is true I understand cart and terce, parry and thrust, but I have heard that Prettyman studied under Olivier. Many a man has outlived the passage of a bullet, or the thrust of a sword through him. But my constitution is so delicate! Curse blast it, death and the devil, I do not know what to do."

Sir William, as soon as he had left lord Martin, repaired to the lodgings of Mr.

Prettyman. After a short general conversation, he began, "My dear friend, here has happened the unluckiest thing in nature. You have made some advances, you know, to the charming Delia." "True," cried Prettyman, "I have bestowed upon her a few condescending glances. *C'est une charmante fille*." "Well," added sir William, "and the whole town gives her to you." "*Parbleu!* the town is very impertinent. There will go two words to that bargain." "My lord Martin, you know, has enlisted himself amongst her admirers." "Pox take the blockhead, I suppose he would marry her. *Bien*. After I have led her a dance, he shall do what he pleases with her." "But," said sir William, "my lord intends to call you to an account." "*Morbleu*," cried Prettyman, "I thought I had been in a land of liberty." "But let me tell you, my lord is very absolute. He has fought some half a dozen duels in his time, and every body is afraid of him." "*J'en suis excede*. 'Pon honour, the girl is not worth fighting for." "Oh," said the malicious wit, "but if you give her up for a few threats, your reputation will be ruined for ever." "*Mon Dieu!* this reputation is a very expensive thing. *Je crois* that every girl is a Helen, never so happy as when people are murdering one another, and towns are fired for her sake. Is this same *milord* absolutely inexorable?"

"I cannot tell," said sir William, "what may be done. If you were to fly, he would pursue you to the ends of the earth. But suppose now you were upon your knees, to retract your pretensions to this silly girl." "*Pardi*" answered Prettyman, "that is damned hard! are you sure his lordship is so compleat a master of the science of defence?" "Nay," replied sir William, "I cannot tell. I believe indeed he never received a wound, but I think I remember to have heard of one duel he fought, in which his antagonist came off with his life." "Ah, *diable l'emporte!* That will not do neither. These bullets are the aukwardest things in the world. Do you think you could not prevail with his Lordship to use only powder?" "Powder," cried sir William, "that is an excellent jest. My lord always loads with six small slugs." "Six slugs! ah the bloody minded villain! It is confounded hard that a gentleman cannot pass through life, without being *degoute* with these unpolished Vandals. *Ah, mon cher ami*, I will put the affair entirely into your hands: do, *pour i'amour de Dieu*, bring me out of this scrape as well as you can." "Well my dear Prettyman, I will exert myself on your account; but, upon my soul, I had rather have an affair with half a regiment of commissioned officers fresh imported from America."

Sir William Twyford, having thus brought the affair to some degree of forwardness, now waited on his lordship. "My dear lord Martin," said he, "what have you resolved upon? The affair is briefly thus--you must either give up Delia, or fight Mr. Prettyman." "Give up Delia!" exclaimed the little lord; "by all that is sacred I will sooner spill the last drop of my blood. But," added he, "what necessity is there for the alternative you propose? True, I fear no man. But to be continually engaged in quarrels would acquire me the character of a desperado." "Indeed," said sir William, "you have been somewhat lavish in those sort of affairs, but I do not see how you can be off in the present instance. Prettyman has heard of the bustle you made about the fellow at the ball, that tricked you of your partner; and he will never pardon the affront, if you pay less attention to him." "Pox take the blockhead, he is mighty nice, methinks, in his temper. I have a great mind not to gratify him." "Oh," cried sir William, "you never had such an opportunity to establish your character for ever. And the fellow I believe is no better than a coward at bottom."

It would be endless to relate all the stratagems of sir William to bring the business to the conclusion he wished. How he terrified the brawny *petit maitre*, and anon he animated the little peer. His lordship felt the force of his friend's eloquence, but even his highest flights of heroism were qualified with temporary misgivings. For poor Mr. Prettyman, he feared to stay, and dared not fly. If he could have forgotten the danger he apprehended, his good natured friend by the studied exaggerations in which he was continually clothing it, would have perfectly succeed in refreshing his memory. But in reality it was never absent from his thoughts. His slumbers were short and disturbed. And he could scarcely close his eyes, ere the enraged lord Martin, with his sword drawn, and his countenance flaming with inexorable fury, presented himself to his affrighted imagination.

At length sir William by his generous interposition affected a compromise. It was agreed that Mr. Prettyman should fall upon his knees before lord Martin in the public room in the presence of Delia, and, asking his pardon, put a small cane into his hand. "My lord," said sir William to the beau, "is as generous as he is brave. He will not make an improper use of the advantage you put into his hands. He will raise you from the humble posture you will have assumed, and, embracing you cordially, all that is past will be forgotten. As his lordship will take you under his protection, not an individual will dare to reflect upon you." "Mr. Prettyman," said sir William to lord Martin, "unites the heart of a chicken to the most absolute skill in the small sword that ever I saw. I have been only capable of restraining him by representing your lordship as the most furious and impracticable of mankind. If he once suspect that I have misrepresented you, a duel, in which I am afraid your lordship would be overmatched, must be the inevitable consequence. Might I therefore presume to advise, your lordship should make use of the advantage I have gained you without mercy."

CHAPTER VI.
Containing some Specimens of Heroism.

The evening now approached, in which the scene sir William Twyford had with so much pains prepared, was to be acted. An imperfect rumour had spread that something extraordinary was to pass in the public room. Miss Prim was of opinion that a duel would be fought. "I shall be frightened out of my wits," said she. "But I must go, for one loves any thing new, and I believe there is nothing in it that a modest woman may not see." Miss Gawky thought it would be a boxing match. "Bless us, my dear lord Martin could stand no chance with that great lubberly macaroni." But Miss Griskin, with a look of more than common sagacity, assured the ladies that she had penetrated to the very bottom of the matter. "Mr. Prettyman and lord Martin have ordered two large rounds of beef to be set upon the table at supper, and they mean to lay about them for a wager."

In this manner every one made her own conjecture, which she preferred to that of all the rest. Curiosity was wrought up to the highest pitch, and the uncertainty that prevailed upon the subject, rendered the affair still more interesting. The rooms were early filled with an uncommon number of spectators. About nine o'clock Mr. Prettyman entered, but instead of exerting himself with his usual vivacity, he retired to one corner of the room, and sat in a sheepish and melancholy posture. Not long after, sir William Twyford and lord Martin came in, arm in arm.

The peer strutted immediately to the upper end of the room. Delia stood near him. "My lovely girl," said he, with an air of vulgar familiarity, "I am rejoiced to see you. I hope I shall one day prove myself worthy of your favour."

While this passed Mr. Prettyman was by no means in an enviable condition. From the operation of fear and vexation he perspired very profusely. Vanity, as we have said, might almost be termed his ruling passion, and he would never have sacrificed it so publicly to any consideration less immediate than that of personal safety. Ardently did he long to have the terrible scene concluded. But he had neither strength nor spirits to advance a step, or even to rise from his seat.

Sir William Twyford now came up to him, and took hold of his hand. "My dear friend," said he, "be not dispirited. It is no more than a flea-bite, and it will be over in a moment. You will acquire the friendship of the first personage in the county, and far from losing any thing in the public esteem, you will be more respected than ever." "*Morbleu*," cried the beau, "my shoulders ake for it already. But, *mon tres cher & tres excellent ami*, do not desert me, and remind the peer of the generosity you talked of."

Sir William now raised him from his seat, and led him to the middle of the room. Lord Martin, with a stately air, advanced a few steps. In spite however of all the heroism he could assume, as the important affair drew towards a crisis, he began to tremble. Mr. Prettyman fell upon his knees, and sir William put a cane into his hand. But in this posture the beau remained still somewhat taller than his antagonist. "Most worthy lord," cried he in a tremulous voice, "I am truly sorry for the misunderstanding that has happened, and I am filled with the most ardent"----While he was yet speaking he advanced the cane in the attitude of presenting it. "Villain," said lord Martin, who between fear and rage could no longer contain himself, and snatched it from his hand. But he could scarcely reach beyond the shoulder of his enemy, and blinded with emotion and exertion, instead of directing his blows as he ought to have done, he struck him two or three very severe strokes on the head and face. The beau bore it as long as he could. But at length bellowing out, "*Mon Dieu, je suis meurtrie*, I am beaten to a jelly," he rose from his knees. His antagonist being between him and the door, he fairly threw him upon his back, and flying out of the room he stopped not till he arrived at the inn, where, ordering his phaeton and six, he ascended without a moment's pause, and drove off for London.

In the mean time, every thing in the public room was in confusion and disorder. Sir William flew to support the discomfited hero, who had received a grievous contusion in his shoulder. Miss Griskin giggled, the other ladies screamed, and Miss Languish, as usual, fainted away. "Bless me," cried Miss Fletcher, "it is the queerest affair"--"By my troth," said Miss Gawky, "it is vastly fine." "But not half so fine," cried Miss Griskin, "as the buttocks of beef."

By this time lord Martin had raised himself in a sitting posture and uttered a deep groan. "Best of friends," said he, pressing the hand of sir William, "tell me truly, am I victorious, or am I defeated?" "Oh *victoria*!" cried sir William; "never heed a slight skin wound that you received in the combat." His lordship stood up. "Damnation, pox confound it!" said he, a little recovering himself, "what is become of the rascal? I have not given him half what he deserved. But, ladies," added he flourishing his cane, "it is my maxim, as I am strong to be merciful."

Saying this, he advanced towards Delia, and, with a flourish of importance and conceit, laid the weapon, which he had so roundly employed, at her feet. "Loveliest of women," said he, "to your shrine I devote myself. Upon your altar, I lay the insignia of my prowess. Deign, gentlest of thy sex, to accept thus publicly of those sighs which I have long poured forth upon thy account."

Delia, though the native modesty of her character caused her whole face to be suffused with blushes at having the eyes of the whole company thus turned upon her, regarded the peer with a look of ineffable disdain, and turned from him in silence.

Such were the transactions of an evening, which will doubtless long be remembered by such as had the good fortune to be spectators. The natural impertinence and insolence of lord Martin were swelled by the event to ten times their natural pitch. He crowed like a cock, and cackled like a goose. The vulgar of the other sex, who are constantly the admirers of success, however unmerited, and conceit, however unfounded, thought his lordship the greatest man in the world. The inequality of his legs was removed by the proof he had exhibited of his prowess. The inequality of his shoulders was hid under a rent-roll of ten thousand a year. And the narrowness of his intellects, the optics of these connoisseurs were not calculated to discern.

The peer, as we have already hinted, was the suitor most favoured by the father of our heroine. The principal passion of the old gentleman was the love of money. But at the same time he was not absolutely incapable of relishing the inferior charms of a venerable title and a splendid reputation. Perceiving that his client continually rose in the public opinion, he was more eager than ever to have the match concluded. Lord Martin, though his organs were not formed to delight in beauty at the first hand, was yet tickled with the conceit of carrying off so fair a prize from the midst of a thousand gaping expectants.

It will naturally be imagined that the situation of Delia at this moment was by no means an enviable one. She was caught in the snares of love. And the more she struggled to get free, she was only the more limed and entangled. The recollection of the hopelessness of her love by no means sufficed to destroy it. The recollection of her former carelessness and gaiety was not able to restore her to present ease. In vain she summoned pride and maiden dignity to support her. In vain she formed resolutions, which were broken as soon as made. Every where she was haunted by the image of her dear unknown. Her nights were sleepless and uneasy. The fire and brightness of her eyes were tarnished. *She pined in green and yellow melancholy.*

The more dear were the ideal image that accompanied her, the more did she execrate and detest her persecutor. "No," cried she, "I will never be his. Never shall the sacred tie, which should only unite congenial spirits, be violated by two souls, distant as the poles, jarring as contending elements. My father may kill me. Alas, of what value is life to me! It is a long scene of unvaried misfortune. It is a dreary vista of despair. He may kill me, but never, never shall he force me to a deed my soul abhors."

CHAPTER VII.

Containing that with which the reader will be acquainted when he has read it.

The cup of misfortune, by which it was decreed that the virtue and the constancy of our heroine should be tried, was not yet ended. The disposition of a melancholy lover is in the utmost degree variable. Now the fair Delia studiously sought to plunge herself in impervious solitude; and now, worn with a train of gloomy reflections, she with equal eagerness solicited the society of her favourite companion.

By this time sir William Twyford and Miss Fletcher were become in a manner inseparable. Of consequence the company of the one necessarily involved that of the other. And the gaiety and good humour of sir William, tempered as they were by an excellent understanding, and an unaffected vein of sportive wit, were the sweetest medicine to the wounded heart of Delia. When she had first chosen Miss Fletcher for her intimate friend, her own faculties had not yet reached their maturity; and habit frequently renders the most insipid amusements pleasurable and interesting. Southampton itself did not afford the largest scope for selection. And however our readers may decide respecting the merit of the easy, the voluble and the good humoured Miss Fletcher, they will scarcely be disposed to deny that of all the female characters we have hitherto exhibited, she was the most amiable.

One evening, as these three friends were sitting together, sir William took occasion to lament the necessity that was laid upon him to quit Southampton for a few days, though he hoped very speedily to be able to return. His inamorata, as usual, was very inquisitive to learn the business that was to deprive her for a time of the presence of a lover, of whom she was not a little ostentatious. Sir William answered that he was under an engagement to be present at the marriage of one of his college friends, and that he should set out in company with Mr. Moreland.

At that name our tender and apprehensive fair one involuntarily started. "Mr. Moreland!" said she to herself, "Ah, it was at his house that my unknown resided. It is very seldom that Mr. Moreland undertakes a journey. Surely there must be something particularly interesting to him in the affair. The strange combination of circumstances terrifies and perplexes me. Would I were delivered from this state of uncertainty! Would to God I were dead!"

The uncertainty which afflicted her was however of a very short duration. Miss Fletcher, by an inexhaustible train of interrogatories, led sir William to relate by degrees every thing he knew of the affair. The young gentleman his friend was the nephew and heir of Mr. Moreland. The present match had been long upon the carpet, and was a very considerable one in point of fortune. "Did the nephew ever visit Mr. Moreland?" "Very frequently," said sir William. "And he is visited" interposed Delia, "by other young gentlemen from the university?" "No," answered sir William. "Mr. Moreland, who is an old batchelor, full of oddities and sensibility, has a general dislike of young collegians. He thinks them pert, dissolute, arrogant, and pedantic. He therefore never receives any but his nephew, for whom he has the most ardent affection, and sometimes by particular grace myself who am his intimate friend." "And how long is it since the young gentleman paid a visit to his uncle?" Sir William looked a little surprized at so particular a question, but answered: "He was here not above a fortnight ago to invite his uncle to the wedding. But he is rather serious and thoughtful in his temper, so that he is seldom seen in public."

It was now but too certain that the friend of sir William, and the amiable unknown, who had made a conquest of the heart of Delia, were the same person. The surprise at which she was taken, and the unwelcome manner in which her doubts were now at once resolved, were too much for the delicate frame of our heroine. She sat for a moment gazing with an eager and unmeaning stare upon the face of sir William. But she presently recollected herself, and, bursting out of the room, flew to her chamber in the same instant, and was relieved by a flood of tears.

Sir William was inexpressibly surprised at this incident. Delia, he was sure, did not even know the name of his friend, and he could scarcely imagine that she had ever seen him. Miss Fletcher, though considerably astonished herself, gave sir William an account of so many particulars of what had passed between his friend and our heroine, as were perfectly sufficient to solve the difficulty. In return the baronet explained to her the exact situation of the affair of Damon, told her that he did not believe the day was yet fixed, and assured her that Mr. Moreland and himself waited for a farther summons, though it must be confessed that it was expected every hour.

These particulars, when communicated to Delia by the indefatigable assiduity of Miss Fletcher, afforded her but a very slender consolation. "What avails it me," said she, "that the day is not fixed? Every considerable circumstance, there is reason to believe, is determined. He marries, with the approbation of all his friends, a lady, my superior in rank and fortune, and who is probably every way worthy of him. Ah, why am I thus selfish and envious? No, let me pine away in obscurity, let me be forgotten. But may he live long and happy. Did he not tell me, that he went to seek the *mistress of his fate*?--And yet," interrupted she, "he accompanied the information with words of such sweet import, with so much tenderness and gentleness, as will never be erased from my mind. Ah foolish girl, wilt thou for ever delude thyself, wilt thou be for ever extracting comfort from despair? No! Long enough hast thou been misguided by the meteor of hope. Long enough hast thou been cheated by the visions of youthful fancy. There is now no remedy left. Let me die."

There were two passions that predominated in the breast of sir William Twyford. The first was that of a humourist, and to this almost every other object was occasionally sacrificed. But he had likewise a large fund of good nature. He perceived, that in two successive instances, however unintentionally, his conduct had been the source of unhappiness to the most amiable of her sex. The victory of lord Martin had put it more than ever in his power to harrass Delia. She was incessantly importuned, now by her father, and now by her inamorato. And her distress, if it had wanted any addition, was rendered compleat by the expected marriage of one, whose personal accomplishments had caught her unwary heart. He lamented the undeserved misfortune of youth and beauty. His heart bled for her.

Thus circumstanced, his active benevolence determined him not to lose a moment, in endeavouring to repair the mischief of which he had so unfortunately been the author. He had never cordially approved of the intended union between his friend and Miss Frampton. She was of the first order of coquettes, and it might have puzzled even an anatomist to determine, whether she had a heart. Descartes informs us that the soul usually resides in the pineal gland, but the soul of this lady seemed to inhabit in her eyes. She had been caught with the figure of Damon. And had a figure more perfectly beautiful, if that had been possible, or an equipage more brilliant, presented itself, he did not doubt but that it would carry away the prize.

Miss Frampton was heiress to a fortune of fifty thousand pounds. The father of Damon, whose soul, in union with some amiable qualities, which served him for a disguise, had the misfortune to be exceedingly mercenary at the bottom, had proposed the match to his son. Damon, who had never in his life been guilty of an act of disobedience, received the recommendation of his father with a prejudice in its favour. He waited upon the young lady and found her beautiful, high spirited, accomplished, and incensed by a thousand worshippers. Her disposition was not indeed congenial to his own. But he was prejudiced by filial duty, dazzled by her charms, and led on insensibly by the mildness and pliableness of his character. In a word, every thing had been concluded, and the wedding was daily expected to take place.

CHAPTER VIII.

Two Persons of Fashion.

In pursuance of the determination he had formed, sir William immediately set out for Oxford, where his friend still resided. As he had lived with him upon terms of the most unreserved familiarity, he made use of the liberty of an intimate, and, without being announced, abruptly entered his chamber. Damon was sitting in a melancholy posture, his countenance dejected, and his eye languid. Upon the entrance of the baronet he looked up, and struck with the sudden appearance of one to whom he was so ardently attached, his visage for a moment assumed an air of gaiety and pleasure.

"Ha," cried sir William, with his wonted spriteliness of accent, "methinks the countenance of my Damon does not bespeak the sentiments that become a bride-groom." "I am afraid not," answered Damon. "But tell me to what am I indebted for this agreeable and unexpected visit?" "We will talk of that another time. But when did you see my play-fellow, Miss Frampton?" "I have not seen her," replied our hero with a sigh half uttered, and half suppressed, "these ten days." "What" cried the baronet, "no misunderstanding, eh?" "Not absolutely that. I saw her, I fear, without all the rapture that becomes a lover, and she resented it with a coldness that did not introduce an immediate explanation. Since that time I have been somewhat indisposed, or probably affairs would now have been settled." "And what," said sir William, "must we apply the old maxim, that the falling out of lovers is the consoli-dating of love?"

Damon from the entrance of his friend had appeared a good deal agitated. He was no longer able to contain himself. He eagerly seized the hand of sir William and clasped it between both of his. "My dear baronet, I have never concealed from you a thought of my heart. But my present situation is so peculiarly delicate and distress-ing, that I can scarcely form any sentiment of it, or even dare trust myself to recol-lect it. I have seen," continued he, "ah, that I could forget it! a woman, beauteous as the day, before whom the charms of Miss Frampton disappear, as, before the rising sun, each little star *hides its diminish'd head*. Her features, full of sensibility, her

voice such as to thrill the soul and all she says, pervaded with wit and good sense."
"And where," cried the baronet, in a lively tone, "resides this peerless she?"

"Alas," answered the disconsolate Damon, "it matters not. I shall see her no more. Virtue, honour, every thing forbids it. I may be unhappy, but I will never deserve to be so. Miss Frampton has my vows. Filial duty calls on me to fulfil them. Obstacles without number, Alps on Alps arise, to impede my prosecution of a fond and unlicensed inclination. The struggle has cost me something, but it is over. I have recovered my health, I have formed my resolution. This very day, (you, my good friend, will accept the apology) I had determined to repair to Beaufort Place. Doubt and uncertainty nourish the lingering distemper that would undo me. I will come to a decision."

Sir William was not of a temper to abdicate any affair in which he had embarked, before success appeared absolutely unattainable. Like Caesar, it was enough for him that the thing appeared possible to be done, to engage him to persevere. He therefore begged leave to accompany his friend, and they set out together that very afternoon.

Beaufort Place, the habitation of Miss Frampton, was only six miles from Oxford. And, as he knew that Sir Harry Eustace, the son of that lady's mother by a second husband, was now upon a visit to his sister, sir William Twyford made no scruple of proceeding with his friend immediately to the house.

After a short general conversation, sir William drew the young baronet into the garden. In the mean time sir Harry's chariot was preparing, as he had fixed the conclusion of his visit for that evening. After an interval of half an hour the servant brought word that the carriage was ready. Sir Harry, who was a young man of little ceremony, bowed *en passant* before the parlour window, and immediately hurried away.

Sir William stood for some time at the door of the house after sir Harry had driven away. Presently he observed another carriage advancing by the opposite road. The liveries were flaunting and the attendants numerous. They drew nearer, and he perceived that it was the equipage of lord Osborne. Since therefore the lovers were to be so soon interrupted by the entrance of a new visitant, he thought proper immediately to enter the parlour.

He had only time to remark the air and countenance of Damon and the young lady. They appeared mutually cold and embarassed. He could trace in his friend the aukwardness and timidity of one who was unused to act a studied part. Miss Frampton, with a countenance uninterested and inattentive, affected the carriage of a person who thought herself insulted.

Lord Osborne was now announced. He was a young nobleman, that had spent a considerable part of his fortune upon the continent. With a narrow understanding and a contracted heart, he had been able by habitual cunning and invincible effrontery, to acquire the reputation of a man of parts. Courage was the only respectable quality, his possession of which could not be questioned. He was a debauchee and a gamester. There was no meanness he had not practised, there was no villainy of which he could not boast. With this character, he was universally respected and courted by all such as wished to acquire the reputation of men of gaiety and spirit. The ladies were all dying for him, as for a man who had ruined more innocence, and occasioned a greater consumption of misery, than any other man in the kingdom.

The face of Miss Frampton visibly brightened the moment his name was articulated. She was all spirits and agitation, though she seemed to feel something aukward in her situation. When he entered the room, she flew half way to meet him, but, suddenly recollecting herself, stopt short. "My dear Miss Frampton," said his lordship, with a familiar and indifferent air, "I cannot stop a moment. I am mortified to death. The most unfortunate man! But I could not live a whole day without seeing you. Believe me to be more impassioned, more ardent than ever." Saying this be directed a slight glance and a half bow towards our two friends. "Farewel, my charmer, my adorable!" said he, and kissed her hand. Miss Frampton struck him a slight blow with her fan, and crying, with an easy wink, "Remember!" she dropt him a profound curtesey and his lordship departed.

For a moment the whole company was silent. "By my soul," exclaimed sir William, "this is the most singular affair!" "Oh, nothing at all," answered the young lady. "It is all *a la mode de Paris*. In France no man of fashion can presume to accost a lady, whether young or old, but in the language of love. But it means no more, than when a minister of state says to his first clerk, *your humble servant*, or to the widow of a poor seaman, *your devoted slave*." "Oh," cried sir William, "that is all. And by my faith, it is mighty pretty. What think you Damon? I hope, when you are married, you will have no objection to lord Osborne, or any other person of fashion making love to your wife before your face." "What an indelicate question!" said Miss Frampton. "I declare, baronet, you are grown an absolute boor. Nobody ever talks of marriage now. A woman of fashion blushes to hear it mentioned before a third person." "Why, to say the truth, madam, I have been honoured with so great an intimacy by Damon, that I thought that might excuse the impropriety. And now, pray your ladyship, must I wait till we are alone, before I ask my friend whether his happy day be fixed?" "Since you will talk," said Miss Frampton, "of the odious subject, I believe I may tell you that it is not. We are in no such hurry." "My dear sweet play-fellow," said the baronet, "I must tell you once for all that I am no adept in French fashions. So that you will give me leave to use the unceremonious language of an Englishman. My friend here, you know, is a little sheepish, but I have words at will. I thought matters had been nearer a termination." "And pray, my good sir, let the gentleman speak for himself. If he is not dissatisfied, why should you be in such haste?" "Indeed, madam," interposed Damon, "I am not perfectly satisfied. Perhaps indeed a lover ought to think himself happy enough in being permitted to dance attendance upon a lady of your charms. But I once thought, madam, that we had advanced somewhat farther." "I cannot tell," answered the lady with an air of levity. "Just as you please. But I cannot see why we should put ourselves to any inconvenience. Lord Osborne"--"Lord Osborne!" interrupted sir William with some warmth, "and pray what has his lordship to do with the matter?" "Really sir William," replied Miss Frampton, "you are very free. But his lordship is my friend, and I hope Damon has no objection to his continuing so." "Look you," answered sir William, "I would neither have lord Osborne for the rival of Damon now, nor for your *chichisbee* hereafter." "And yet I am not sure," cried she, "that he may not be both." "Is there then," said the baronet, "no engagement subsisting between you and Damon?" "I believe," cried Miss Frampton, a little hesitating, "there may be something of the kind. But we may change our minds you know, and I do not think that I shall prosecute upon it. Ha! ha! ha!" "To say the truth," replied sir William, "I believe lord Osborne is not only the rival of Damon, but a very formidable one too. But let me tell you, Bella, a character so respectable as that of my friend, and so true an Englishman, must not be allowed to dance attendance." "As he pleases. I believe we understand one another. And to say the truth at once, perhaps some time hence I may have no aversion to lord Osborne."

The reader will not suppose that the conversation continued much longer. Damon and the young lady came to a perfect understanding, and parted without any very ungovernable desire of seeing each other again. And thus by the gay humour and active friendship of sir William Twyford, an affair was happily terminated, which, from the timidity and gentleness of our hero, might otherwise have lingered several months to the mutual dissatisfaction of both parties. Damon quitted the house in raptures, and was no sooner seated in the chariot, than he pressed his friend repeatedly to his breast, and committed a thousand extravagancies of joy.

CHAPTER IX.
A tragical Resolution.

Damon and his friend spent the evening together in the chambers of our hero. They now discussed a variety of those subjects, which naturally arise between friends who have been for any time separated. Damon threw aside that reserve which the consciousness of a fault had hitherto involuntarily imposed upon him, and related more explicitly who the lady was of whom he was so much enamoured, and in what manner he had first seen her. Recollecting that the baronet was just returned from the environs of Southampton, he eagerly enquired into the health and situation of his mistress.

Sir William related to him the adventure of Mr. Prettyman, as we have already stated it to our readers, and deeply lamented the persecution to which Delia was subjected from the haughty victor. "And is there," cried Damon eagerly, "no prospect of his lordship's success?" "I believe," answered sir William, "that he is of all men her mortal aversion." "And is there no happy lover in all her train, that she regards with a partial eye?" "None," replied the baronet, "she is chaste as snow, and firm as mountain oaks." "Propitious coldness!" exclaimed Damon, "for that may heaven send down a thousand blessings on her head!"

"But you talked," added he, "of some occasion of your journey which you deferred relating to me." "The occasion," answered sir William, determined to preserve inviolate the secret of Delia, "is already fulfilled. I heard from young Eustace of the appearance and addresses of Osborne, and suspecting the rest, I determined to deliver you from the clutches of a girl whom I always thought unworthy of you. And now" added he cheerfully, "free as the winds, we can pursue uncontrolled the devices of our own hearts."

The next morning the two friends proceeded to the house of lord Thomas Villiers, the father of Damon. He had already learned something of the visits of lord Osborne at Beaufort Place. He was not therefore much surprised to hear of the scene, which had passed between his son and the lady of that mansion. But there was something more to be done, in order to gain the approbation of the father to the new project, in the prosecution of which both these friends were equally sanguine.

Lord Thomas Villiers was, as we have already said, avaricious. He was not therefore much pleased with the proposal of a match with a lady, whose fortune was not the half of that of Miss Frampton. He was tinctured with the pride of family, and he could not patiently think for a moment, of marrying his only son to the daughter of a tradesman. Sir William employed all his eloquence, and accommodated himself with infinite dexterity to the humours of the person with whom he had to deal. Damon indeed said but little, but his looks expressed more, than the baronet, with all his abilities, and all his friendship, was able to suggest. In spite of both, the father continued inexorable.

The mind of Damon was impressed with the most exalted ideas upon the subject of filial duty. Had his heart been pre-engaged, before the affair of Miss Frampton was proposed to him, he might not perhaps have carried his complaisance so far, as to have married the indifferent person, in spite of all his views and all his prepossessions. But in his estimate, the actual entering into a connection for life in opposition to the will of a parent, was a mode of conduct very different from, and far more exceptionable than the refusing to unite oneself with a person in whose society one had not the smallest reason to look for happiness.

There was another inducement that had much weight with Damon, and even with his more sanguine friend, sir William Twyford. The fortune neither of Damon nor Delia was independent. Lord Thomas Villiers was filled with too many prepossessions and too much pride, easily to retract an opinion he had once adopted, or to forgive an opposition to his judgment. The narrow education of a tradesman it was natural to suppose had rendered the mind of Mr. Hartley still more tenacious, and unmanageable. And neither would sir William have been willing to see his friend, nor would the lover readily have involved his mistress in circumstances of pecuniary distress.

The resolution of Damon was therefore speedily taken. Every motive that could have weight, served to counteract the bias of his inclination. He by no means wanted either firmness or spirit. He resolved to struggle, nor to cease his efforts till he had conquered. With this design he entreated, and, after some difficulties, obtained of his father leave to enter himself in the army, and to make a campaign in America.

The character of his heart seemed particularly formed for military pursuits. He was grave and thoughtful, he was generous and humane. To a mind contemplative and full of sensibility, he united a temper, frank, open, and undisguised. He was usually mild, gentle and pliant. But in a situation, that called for determination and spirit, it was impossible to appear more bold and manly, more cool and decided,--Affectionate was the farewel of his father, and still more affectionate that of his friend. Damon, though he endeavoured to summon all his resolution, could not restrain a sigh when he considered himself as about to sail for distant climates, and recollected, that probably, before his return, his beloved mistress, *dearer than life and all its joys*, would be united, irrevocably united to another. But here we must take leave of our hero, and return to his fair inamorata.

PART the SECOND.

CHAPTER I.

In which the Story begins over again.

Sir William Twyford had taken care to inform Miss Fletcher, and by her means Delia herself, of every circumstance as it occurred. Delia was indeed flattered by the breach that had taken place with Miss Frampton, and the perfect elucidation, which the story of this lady afforded to the most enigmatical expressions of Damon, in the interesting scene that had passed between them in the alcove. She no longer doubted of the reality of his attachment. Her heart was soothed, and her pride secretly flattered, in recollecting that she had not suffered herself to be caught by one who was perfectly indifferent to her.

But the information that stifled all her hopes, and gave her the prospect of so long, and, too probably, an eternal absence, sat heavy upon her spirits, and preyed upon her delicate constitution. From the persecutions of lord Martin she had no respite. Her eye grew languid, the colour faded in her damask cheek, and her health visibly decayed.

At this time Miss Fletcher proposed a journey to Windsor and other places, and intreated to have her friend to accompany her. Mr. Hartley, with all his foibles, was much attached to his only child, and deeply afflicted with the alteration he perceived in her. He readily therefore gave his consent to the proposed jaunt. "When she returns, it will be time enough," said he to lord Martin, "to bring things to the conclusion, so much desired by both of us. I will not put my darling into your hands, but with that health and gaiety, which have so long been the solace of my old age, and which cannot fail to make any man happy that deserves her."

Delia set out without any other inclination, than to escape from intreaties that were become in the highest degree disagreeable to her. She was addressed no longer upon a topic, of which she wished never to hear. Her eye was no longer wounded with the sight of her insolent admirer. This had an immediate and a favourable effect upon her. The conversation of Miss Fletcher was lively and unflagging, and the simplicity of her remarks proved an inexhaustible source of entertainment to our heroine.

They travelled leisurely and visited a variety of parks and seats of noblemen which lay in their way. The taste of Delia was delicate and refined. A continual succession of objects; gardens, architecture, pictures and statues soothed her spirits, and gradually restored her to that gaiety and easiness of temper, which had long rendered her the most lovely and engaging of her sex.

At length they arrived at Windsor. The simple dignity of the castle, its commanding situation, and the beautiful effects of the river from below, rendered it infinitely the most charming spot our heroine had yet seen. Her spirits were on the wing, she was all life and conversation, and the most constant heart, that nature had ever produced, for a moment, forgot her hopes, her fears, her inclinations, and her Damon.

She was now standing at a window that commanded the terrace. The evening was beautiful, and the walk crouded. There were assembled persons of all sexes and of different ranks. All appeared gaiety and splendour. The supple courtier and the haughty country gentleman seemed equally at their ease. There was thoughtless youth and narrative old age. The company passed along, and object succeeded object without intermission.

One of the last that caught the eye of Delia, was that of two gentlemen walking arm in arm, and seeming more grave than the rest of the company. They were both tall and well shaped; but one of them had somewhat more graceful and unembarrassed in his manner than the other. The latter was dressed in black, the former in colours, with much propriety and elegance.

As they turned at the end of the walk the eye of Delia caught in the latter the figure of Damon. She was inexpressibly astonished, she trembled in every limb, and could scarcely support herself to a seat. Miss Fletcher had caught the same object at the same moment, and, though she probably might not otherwise have been clear in her recollection, the disorder of Delia put her conjecture out of doubt. She therefore, before our heroine had time to recollect herself, dispatched her brother, who had attended them in their journey, to inform Damon that a lady in the castle was desirous to speak with him.

In an instant our hero and his companion, escorted by young Fletcher, entered the room. The astonishment of Damon, at being so suddenly introduced to a person, whom he had never expected to see again, was immeasurable. He rushed forward with a kind of rapture; he suddenly recollected himself; but at length advanced with hesitation. There was no one present beside those we have already named. The castle was probably familiar to every person except Delia and her companions. Every one beside was therefore assembled upon the terrace.

Our heroine now gradually recovered from the disorder into which the unexpected sight of Damon had thrown her. She was much surprised at looking up to find him in her presence. "How is this," cried she, "how came you hither?" "The meeting," said our hero, "is equally unexpected to us both. But, ah, my charmer, whence this disorder? Why did you tremble, why look so pale?" "Oh goodness," cried Miss Fletcher, "what should it be? Why it was nothing in all the world, but her seeing you just now from the window." "And were you," cried Damon eagerly, "so kind as to summon me to your presence?" "No, no, my good sir," said the lively lady, "you must thank me for that". "How then at least," said the lover, "must I interpret your disorder?"

Delia was inexpressibly confused at the inconsiderate language of her companion. "I cannot tell," said she, "you must not ask me. You must forget it." "And can I," cried Damon with transport, "ever forget a disorder so propitious, so flattering? Can I hope that the heart of my charmer is not indifferent to her Damon!" "Oh sir, be silent. Do not use a language like this." "Alas," cried he, "too long has my passion been suppressed. Too long have I been obliged to act a studied part, and employ a language foreign to my heart." "I thought," answered Delia, with hesitation, "that you were going to leave the kingdom." "And did my fair one condescend to employ a thought upon me? Did she interest herself in my concern and enquire after my welfare? And how so soon could she have learned my intention?"

This question, joined with the preceding circumstances, completed the confusion of Delia. She blushed, stammered, and was silent. Damon, during this interval, gazed upon her with unmingled rapture. Every symptom she betrayed of confusion, was to him a symptom of something inexpressibly soothing. "Ah," whispered he to himself, "I am beloved, and can I then leave the kingdom? Can I quit this inestimable treasure? Can I slight so pure a friendship, and throw away the jewel upon which all my future happiness depends?"

The conversation, from the peculiar circumstances of the lovers, had so immediately become interesting, that the gentlemen had not had an opportunity of quitting them. During the short silence that prevailed the friend of Damon took young Fletcher by the hand, and led him into the garden. The lovers were now under less restraint. Delia, perceiving that she could no longer conceal her sentiments, confessed them with ingenuous modesty. Damon on the other hand was ravished at so unexpected a discovery, and in a few minutes had lived an age in love.

He now began to recollect himself. "Where," said he, "are all my resolutions? What are become of all the plans I had formed, and the designs in which I had embarked? What an unexpected revolution? No," said he, addressing himself to Delia, "I will never quit you. Do thou but smile, and let all the world beside abandon me. Can you forgive the sacrilegious intention of deserting you, of flying from you to the extremities of the globe? Oh, had I known a thought of Damon had harboured in one corner of your heart, I would sooner have died." "And do you think," cried Delia, "that I will tempt you to disobedience? No. Obey the precepts of your father and your own better thoughts. Heaven designed us not for each other. Neither your friends nor mine can ever be reconciled to the union. Go then and forget me. Go and be happy. May your sails be swelled with propitious gales! May victory and renown attend your steps!" "Ah cruel Delia, and do you wish to banish me? Do you enjoin upon me the impracticable talk, to forget all that my heart holds dear? And will my Delia resign herself to the arms of a more favoured lover?" "Never," cried she with warmth. "I will not disobey my father. I will not marry contrary to his inclinations. But even the authority of a parent shall not drag me to the altar with a man my soul detests." "Propitious sounds! Generous engagements! Thus let me thank thee."--And he kissed her hand with fervour. "Thus far," cried Delia, "I can advance. I employ no disguise. I confess to you all my weakness. Perhaps I ought to blush. But never will I have this reason to blush, for that my love has injured the object it aspires to bless. Go in the path of fortune. Deserve success and happiness by the exemplariness of your duty. And may heaven shower down blessings without number!"

CHAPTER II.

The History of Mr. Godfrey.

In expostulations like these our lovers spent their time without coming to any conclusion, till the evening and Miss Fletcher warned them that it was time to depart. Damon was to proceed for London early the next morning. He therefore intreated of Delia to permit his friend Mr. Godfrey, who was obliged to continue in the place some days longer, to wait upon her with his last commands. He informed himself of the time when she was to return to Southampton, and he trusted to be there not long after her. In the mean time, as his situation was at present very precarious, he prevailed upon her to permit him to write to her from time to time, and to promise to communicate to him in return any thing of consequence that might happen to herself.

During the remainder of the evening Miss Fletcher made several ingenious observations upon what had passed. Delia gently blamed her for having so strangely occasioned the interview, though in reality she was by no means displeased by the event it had produced. "Bless us, child, you are as captious as any thing. Why I would not but have seen it for ever so much. Well, he is a sweet dear man, and so kind, and so polite, for all the world I think him just such another as Mr. Prattle. But then he is grave, and makes such fine speeches, it does one's heart good to hear him. I vow I wish I had such a lover. Sir William never says any thing half so pretty. Bless us, my dear, *he* talks about love, just as if he were talking about any thing else."

The next morning after breakfast, Mr. Godfrey appeared. He brought from Damon a thousand vows full of passion and constancy. He had parted, he said, more determined not to leave England, more resolute to prosecute his love than ever.

Having discharged his commission, he offered his service to escort the ladies in any party they might propose for the present day. He said, that being perfectly acquainted with Windsor and its environs, he flattered himself he might be able to contribute to their entertainment. The very gallant manner in which this offer was made, determined Miss Fletcher, as something singular and interesting in the appearance of Mr. Godfrey did our heroine, cheerfully to close with the proposal.

The person of Mr. Godfrey as we have already said was tall and genteel. There was a diffidence in his manner, that seemed to prove that he had not possessed the most extensive acquaintance with high life; but he had a natural politeness that amply compensated for the polish and forms of society. His air was serious and somewhat melancholy; but there was a fire and animation in his eye that was in the highest degree striking.

Delia engaged him to talk of the character and qualities of Damon. Upon this subject, Mr. Godfrey spoke with the warmth of an honest friendship. He represented Damon as of a disposition perfectly singular and unaccommodated to what he stiled "the debauched and unfeeling manners of the age." He acknowledged with readiness and gratitude, that he owed to him the most important obligations. By degrees Delia collected from him several circumstances of a story, which she before apprehended to be interesting. She observed, that, as he shook off the embarrassment of a first introduction, his language became fluent, elegant, pointed, and even sometimes poetical. Since however he related his own story imperfectly and by piece meal, we shall beg leave to state it in our own manner. And we the rather do it, as we apprehend it to be interesting in itself, and as we foresee that he will make a second appearance in the course of this narrative. We will not however deprive our readers of the reflections he threw out upon the several situations in which he had been placed. We will give them without pretending to decide how far they may be considered as just and well-founded.

Mr. Godfrey was not born to affluent circumstances. At a proper age he had been placed at the university of Oxford, and here it was that he commenced his acquaintance with Damon. At Oxford his abilities had been universally admired. His public exercises, though public exercises by their very nature ought to be dull, had in them many of those sallies, by which his disposition was characterised, and much of that superiority, which he indisputably possessed above his contemporaries. But though admired, he was not courted. In our public places of education, a wide distance is studiously preserved between young men of fortune, and young men that have none. But Mr. Godfrey had a stiffness and unpliableness of temper, that did not easily bend to the submission that was expected of him. He could neither flatter a blockhead, nor pimp for a peer. He loved his friend indeed with unbounded warmth, and it was impossible to surpass him in generousness and liberality. But he had a proud integrity, that whispered him, with, a language not to be controled, that he was the inferior of no man.

He was destined for the profession of a divine, and, having finished his studies, retired upon a curacy of forty pounds a year. His ambition was grievously mortified at the obscurity in which he was plunged; and his great talents, in spite of real modesty, forcibly convinced him, that this was not the station for which nature had formed him. But he had an enthusiasm of virtue, that led him for a time to overlook these disadvantages. "I am going," said he, "to dwell among scenes of unvitiated nature. I will form the peasant to generosity and sentiment. I will teach laborious industry to look without envy and without asperity upon those above them. I will be the friend and the father of the meanest of my flock. I will give sweetness and beauty to the most rugged scenes. The man, that banishes envy and introduces contentment; the man, that converts the little circle in which he dwells into a terrestrial paradise, that renders men innocent here, and happy for ever, may be obscure, may be despised by the superciliousness of luxury; but it shall never be said that he has been a blank in creation. The Supreme Being will regard him with a complacency, which he will deny to kings, that oppress, and conquerors, that destroy the work of his hands."

Such were the suggestions of youthful imagination. But Mr. Godfrey presently found the truth of that maxim, as paradoxical as it is indisputable, that the heart of man is naturally hard and unamiable. He conducted himself in his new situation with the most unexceptionable propriety, and the most generous benevolence. But there were men in his audience, men who loved better to criticise, than to be amended; and women, who felt more complacency in scandal, than eulogium. He displeased the one by disappointing them; it was impossible to disappoint the other. He laboured unremittedly, but his labours returned to him void. "And is it for this," said he, "that I have sacrificed ambition, and buried talents? Is humility to be rewarded only with mortification? Is obscurity and retirement the favourite scene of uneasiness, ingratitude, and impertinence? They shall be no longer my torment. In no scene can I meet with a more scanty success."

He now obtained a recommendation to be private tutor to the children of a nobleman. This nobleman was celebrated for the politeness of his manners and the elegance of his taste. It was his boast and his ambition to be considered as the patron of men of letters. With his prospect therefore in this connection, Mr. Godfrey was perfectly satisfied. "I shall no longer," said he, "be the slave of ignorance, and the victim of insensibility. My talents perhaps point me a step higher than to the business of forming the minds of youth. But, at least, the youth under my care are destined to fill the most conspicuous stations in future life. If propitious fortune might have raised me to the character of a statesman; depressed by adversity, I may yet have the honour of moulding the mind, and infusing generosity into the heart, of a future statesman. I have heard the second son of my patron celebrated for the early promises of capacity. To unfold the springing germs of genius, to direct them in the path of general happiness, is an employment by no means unworthy of a philosopher."

In this situation Mr. Godfrey however once more looked for pleasure, and found disappointment. The nobleman had more the affectation of a patron, than any real enthusiasm in the cause of literature. The abilities of Mr. Godfrey were universally acknowledged. And so long as the novelty remained, he was caressed, honoured, and distinguished. In a short time however, he was completely forgotten by the patron, in the hurry of dissipation, and the pursuits of an unbounded ambition. His eldest care was universally confessed stupid and impracticable. And in the younger he found nothing but the prating forwardness of a boy who had been flattered, without sentiment, and without meaning. Her ladyship treated Mr. Godfrey with superciliousness, as an intruder at her lord's table. The servants caught the example, and showed him a distinction of neglect, which the exquisiteness of his sensibility would not permit him to despise.

Mortified, irritated, depressed, he now quitted his task half finished and threw himself upon the world. "The present age," said he, "is not an age in which talents are overlooked, and genius depressed." He had heard much of the affluence of writers, a Churchil, a Smollet, and a Goldsmith, who had depended upon that only for their support. He saw the celebrated Dr. Johnson caressed by all parties, and acknowledged to be second to no man, whatever were his rank, however conspicuous his station. Full of these ideas, he soon completed a production, fraught with the fire and originality of genius, pointed in its remarks, and elegant in its style. He had now to experience vexations, of which he had before entertained no idea. He carried his work from bookseller to bookseller, and was every where refused. His performance was not seasoned to the times, he was a person that nobody knew, and he had no man of rank, by his importunities and eloquence, to force him into the ranks of fashion. At length he found a bookseller foolish enough to undertake it. But he presently perceived that the gentlemen at the head of that profession were wiser than he. All the motives they had mentioned, and one more, operated against him. The monarchs of the critic realm scouted him with one voice, because his work, was not written in the same cold, phlegmatic insupportable manner as their own.

He had now advanced however too far to retreat. He had too much spirit to resume either of those professions, which for reasons so cogent in his opinion, he had already quitted. He wrote essays, squibs, and pamphlets for an extemporary support. But though these were finished with infinite rapidity, he found that they constituted a very precarious means of subsistence. The time of dinner often came, before the production that was to purchase it was completed; and when completed, it was frequently several days before it could find a purchaser. And his copy money and his taylor's bill were too little proportioned to one another.

He now recollected, what in the gaiety of hope he had forgotten, that *many a flower* only blows, with its sweetness to refresh the *air of a desert*. He recollected many instances of works, raised by the breath of fashion to the very pinnacle of reputation, that sunk as soon again. He recollected instances scarcely fewer, of works, exquisite in their composition, pregnant with beauties almost divine, that had passed from the press without notice. Many had been revived by the cooler and more deliberate judgment of a future age; and more had been lost for ever. The instance of Chatterton, as a proof that the universal patronage of genius was by no means the virtue of his contemporaries, flashed in his face. And he looked forward to the same fate at no great distance, as his own.

To Mr. Godfrey however, fortune was in one degree more propitious. Damon was among the few whose judgment was not guided by the dictate of fashion. Having met accidentally with the performance we have mentioned, he was struck with its beauties. As he had heard nothing of it in the politest circles, he concluded, with his usual penetration, that the author of it was in obscure and narrow circumstances. *Open as day to sweet humanity*, interested warmly in the fortune of the writer of so amiable a performance, he flew to his bookseller's with the usual enquiries. The bookseller stared, and had it not been for the splendour of his dress, and his gilded chariot, would have been tempted to smile at so unfashionable and absurd a question. He soon however obtained the information he desired. And his eagerness was increased, when the name of Godfrey, and the recollection of the talents by which he had been so eminently distinguished, led him to apprehend that he was one, to whose abilities and character he had been greatly attached.

He found some difficulty to obtain admission. But this was quickly removed, as, from the dignity of his appearance, it was not probable that he was a person, from whom Mr. Godfrey had any thing to apprehend. He found him in a wretched apartment, his hair dishevelled and his dress threadbare and neglected. Mr. Godfrey was unspeakably surprised at his appearance. And it was with much difficulty that Damon prevailed upon him to accept of an assistance, that he assured him should be but temporary, if it were in the power of him, or any of his connections, to render him respectable and independent, in such a situation as himself should chuse.

Disappointment and misfortune are calculated to inspire asperity into the gentlest heart. Mr. Godfrey inveighed with warmth, and sometimes with partiality, against the coldness and narrowness of the age. He said, "that men of genius, in conspicuous stations, had no feeling for those whom nature had made their brothers; and that those who had risen from obscurity themselves, forgot the mortifications of their earlier life, and did not imitate the generous justice which had enabled them to fulfil the destination of nature." But though misfortune had taught him asperity upon certain subjects, it had not corrupted his manners, debauched his integrity, or narrowed his heart. He had still the same warmth in the cause of virtue, as in days of the most unexperienced simplicity. He still dreaded an oath, and reverenced the divinity of innocence. He still believed in a God, and was sincerely attached to his honour, though he had often been told, that this was a prejudice, unworthy of his comprehension of thinking upon all other subjects.

CHAPTER III.
A Misanthrope.

Such was the story, in its most essential circumstances, that Mr. Godfrey related. Delia was exceedingly interested in the gaiety of his imagination, the cruelty of his disappointments, and the acuteness, and goodness of heart that appeared in his reflections. Miss Fletcher listened to the whole with gaping wonder. But as soon as he was gone, she began with her usual observations. "Well," said she, "I never saw an author before. I could not have thought that he could have looked like a gentleman. Why, I vow, I could sometimes have taken him for a beau. Ay, but then he talked for all the world as if it had been written in a book. Well, by my troth, it was a mighty pretty story. But I should have liked it better, if there had been a sighing nymph, or a duel or two in it. But do you think it was all of his own making?"

We will not trouble the reader to accompany our ladies from stage to stage during the remainder of their journey. Nothing more remarkable happened, and in ten days they arrived again at Southampton.

Damon met Mr. Moreland in London, and, with that simplicity and candour by which he was distinguished, related to him every circumstance of his story. Mr. Moreland had no predilection in favour of lord Thomas Villiers. His sister, whom he esteemed in all respects an amiable woman, had by no means lived happily with her husband. Avarice and pride of rank were the farthest in the world from being the foibles of Mr. Moreland, and the sensibility of his disposition did not permit him to treat the faults, to which himself was a stranger, with much indulgence. He therefore encouraged Damon to persevere in the pursuit of his inclination, and invited him to return with him into the country. He promised himself to propose the match to Mr. Hartley, and assured his nephew, that he should never feel any narrowness in his circumstances, in case of his father's displeasure, while it was in his power to render them affluent.

In pursuit of this plan, Damon, Mr. Moreland, and sir William Twyford, whom they found in London, and whose goodness of humour led him heartily to approve of the alteration in the plan of his friend, arrived, almost as soon as our travellers, in the neighbourhood of Southampton. Sir William and Damon, soon waited upon their respective mistresses, and in company so mutually acceptable, time sped with a greater velocity than was usual to him, and days appeared no more than hours.

It was impossible that such a connexion should pass long unnoticed. It must be confessed however that it met with no interruption from lord Martin. Perhaps it might have escaped his notice, though it escaped that of no other person. Perhaps he was satiated with the glory he had acquired, and having conquered one beau, would not, like Alexander, have sighed, if there had remained no other beau to conquer. Perhaps the countenance of Mr. Hartley, of which he considered himself as securer than ever, led him, like a wise general, to reflect, that in staking his life against that of a lover, whose chance of success was almost wholly precluded, he mould make a very unfair and unequal combat.

Be this as it will, Mr. Hartley had no such motives to overlook this new occurrence. Just however as he had begun to take it into his mature consideration, he received the compliments of Mr. Moreland, with an intimation of his design to make him a visit that very afternoon.

At this message Mr. Hartley was a good deal surprised. Mr. Moreland he had never but once seen, and in that visit, he thought he had had reason to be offended with him. If that gentleman treated the company of Mr. Prattle and lord Martin, persons universally admired, as not good enough for him, it seemed unaccountable that he should have recourse to him. He was neither distinguished by the elegance of his accomplishments, nor did he much pride himself in the attainments of literature. After many conjectures, he at length determined with infinite sagacity, to suspend his judgement, till Mr. Moreland mould solve the enigma.

This determination was scarcely made before his visitor arrived. That gentleman, who, though full of sensibility and benevolence, was not a man of empty ceremony, immediately opened his business. Mr. Hartley, drew himself up in his chair, and, with the dignity of a citizen of London, who thinks that the first character in the world, cried, "Well, sir, and who is this nephew of yours? I think I never heard of him." "He is the son," answered Mr. Moreland, "of lord Thomas Villiers." "Lord Thomas Villiers! Then I suppose he is a great man. And pray now, sir, if this great man has a mind that his son should marry my daughter, why does he not come and tell me so himself?" "Why in truth," said the other, "lord Thomas Villiers has no mind. But my nephew is his only son, and therefore cannot be deprived of the principal part of his estate after his death. In the mean time, I will take care that he shall have an income perfectly equal to the fortune of Miss Hartley." "You will sir! And so in the first place, this young spark would have me encourage him in disobedience, which is the greatest crime upon God's earth, and in the second, he thinks that I, Bob Hartley, as I sit here, will marry my daughter into any family that is too proud to own us." "As to that, sir," said Moreland, "you must judge for yourself. The young gentleman is an unexceptionable match, and I, sir, whose fortune and character I flatter myself are not inferior to that of any gentleman in the county, shall always be proud to own and receive the young lady." "Why as to that, to be sure, you may be in the right for *auft* that I know. But *howsomdever*, my daughter, do you see, is already engaged to lord Martin." "I should have thought," replied Moreland, "that objection might have been stated in the first instance, without any reflexions upon the conduct and family of the young gentleman. But are you sure that lord Martin is the man of your daughter's choice?" "I cannot say that I ever *axed* her, for I do not see what that has to do with the matter. Lord Martin, do you see, is a fine young man, and a fine fortune. And Delia is my own daughter, and if she should boggle about having him, I would cut her off with a shilling." "Sir," answered Moreland, with much indignation, "that is a conduct that would deserve to be execrated. My nephew, without any sinister means, is master of your daughter's affection; and lord Martin, I have authority to tell you, is her aversion." "Oh, ho! is it so. Well then, sir, I will tell you what I shall do. Your nephew shall never have my daughter, though she had but a rag to her tail. And as for her affections and her aversion, I will lock her up, and keep her upon bread and water, till she knows, that she ought to have neither, before her own father has told her *what is what*." Mr. Moreland, all of whose nerves were irritated into a fever by so much vulgarity, and such brutal insensibility, could retain his seat no longer. He started up, and regarding his entertainer with a look of ineffable indignation, flung the door in his face, and retreated to his chariot.

CHAPTER IV.

Much ado about nothing.

Damon was inexpressibly afflicted at the success of his uncle's embassy. When Mr. Moreland related to him the particulars of his visit, Damon recollected the opposite tempers of the two gentlemen, and blamed himself for not having foreseen the event. Mr. Hartley was infinitely exasperated at the cavalierness with which he had been treated. He now discovered the true cause of his daughter's pertinacity, and proceeded with more vigour than ever.

"And so," cried he, "you have dared to engage your affections without my privity, have you? A pretty story truly. And you would disgrace me for ever, by marrying into the family of a lord, that despises us, and an old fellow, that for half a word would knock your father's brains out." "Indeed sir," replied Delia, "I never thought of marrying without your consent. I only gave the young gentleman leave to ask it of you." "You gave him leave! And pray who are you? And so you was in league with him to send this fellow to abuse me?" "Upon my word, I was not. And I am very sorry if Mr. Moreland has behaved improperly." "*If* Mr. Moreland! and so you pretend to doubt of it! But, let me tell you, I have provided you a husband, worth fifty of this young prig, and I will make you think so." "Indeed sir, I can never think so." "You cannot. And pray who told you to object, before I have named the man. Why, child, lord Martin has ten thousand pounds a year, and is a peer, and is not ashamed of us one bit in all the world." "Alas, sir, I can never have lord Martin. Do not mention him. I am in no hurry. I will live single as long as you please." "Yes, and when you have persuaded me to that, you will jump out at window the next day to this ungracious rascal." "Oh pray sir do not speak so. He is good and gentle." "Why, hussey, am I not master in my own house? I shall have a fine time of it indeed, if I must give you an account of my words." "Sir," said Delia, "I will never marry without your consent." "That is a good girl, no more you shall. And I will lock you up upon bread and water, if you do not consent to marry who I please."

The despotic temper of Mr. Hartley led him to treat his daughter with considerable severity. He suffered her to go very little abroad, and employed every precaution in his power, to prevent any interview between her and her lover. He tried every instrument in turn, threats, promises, intreaties, blustering, to bend her to his will. And when he found that by all these means he made no progress; as his last resource, he fixed a day at no great distance, when he assured her he would be disappointed no longer, and she should either voluntarily or by force yield her hand to lord Martin.

During these transactions, the communication between Delia and her lover was, with no great difficulty, kept open by the instrumentality of their two friends. They scarcely dared indeed to think of seeing each other, as in case this were discovered, Delia would be subject to still greater restraint, and the intercourse, between her and Miss Fletcher, be rendered more difficult. In one instance however, this lady ventured to procure the interview so ardently desired by both parties.

Damon made use of this opportunity to persuade his mistress to an elopement. "You have already carried," said he, "your obedience to the utmost exremity. You have tried every means to bend the inflexible will of your father. If not for my sake then, at least for your own, avoid the crisis that is preparing for you. You detect the husband that your father designs you. If united to him, you confess you must be miserable. But who can tell, in the midst of persons inflexibly bent upon your ruin, no friend at hand to support you, your Damon banished and at a distance, what may be the event? You will hesitate and tremble, your father will endeavour to terrify you into submission, the odious peer will force from you your hand. If, in that moment, your heart should misgive you, if one faultering accent belie the sentiments you have so generously avowed for me, what, ah, what! may be the consequence? No, my fair one, fly, instantly fly. No duty forbids. You have done all that the most rigid moralist could demand of you. Put yourself into my protection. I will not betray your confidence. You shall be as much mistress as ever of all your actions. If you distrust me, at least chuse our common friends sir William Twyford. Chuse any protector among the numerous friends, that your beauty and your worth have raised you. I had rather sacrifice my own prospects of felicity forever, than see the smallest chance that you should be unhappy."

Such were the arguments, which, with all the eloquence of a friend, and all the ardour of a lover, our hero urged upon his mistress. But the gentleness of Delia was not yet sufficiently roused by the injuries she had received, to induce her, to cast off all the ties which education and custom had imposed upon her, and determine upon so decisive a step. "Surely," said she, "there is some secret reward, some unexpected deliverance in reserve, for filial simplicity. Oh, how harsh, how bold, how questionable a step, is that to which you would persuade me! Circumstanced in this manner, the fairest reputation might provoke the tongue of scandal, and the most spotless innocence open a door to the blast of calumny. I will not say that such a step may not be sometimes justifiable. I will not say to what I may myself be urged. But oh, how unmingled the triumph, how sincere the joy if, by persevering in a conduct, in which the path of duty is too palpable to be mistaken, propitious fate may rather grant me the happiness after which I aspire, than I be forced, as it were, myself to wrest it from the hands of providence!"

Such was the result of this last and decisive interview. Delia could not be moved from that line of conduct, upon which she had so virtuously resolved. And Damon having in vain exerted all the rhetoric of which he was master, now gave way to the gloomy suggestions of despair, and now flattered himself with the gleams of hope. He sometimes thought, that Delia might yet be induced to adopt the plan he had proposed; and sometimes he gave way to the serene confidence she expressed, and indulged the pleasing expectation, that virtue would not always remain without its reward.

CHAPTER V.

A Woman of Learning.

We are now brought, in the course of our story, to the memorable scene at Miss Cranley's. "Miss Cranley's!" exclaims one of our readers, in a tone of admiration. "Miss Cranley's!" cries another, "and pray who is she?"

I distribute my readers into two classes, the indolent and the supercilious, and shall accordingly address them upon the present occasion. To the former I have nothing more to say, than to refer them back to the latter part of Chapter I., Part I. where, my dear ladies, you will find an accurate account of the character of two personages, who it seems you have totally forgotten.

To the supercilious I have a very different story to tell. Most learned sirs, I kiss your hands. I acknowledge my error, and throw myself upon your clemency. You see however, gentlemen, that you were somewhat mistaken, when you imagined that I, like my fair patrons, the indolent, had quite lost these characters from my memory.

To speak ingenuously, I did indeed suppose, as far as I could calculate the events of this important narrative beforehand, that the Miss Cranleys would have come in earlier, and have made a more conspicuous figure, than they now seem to have any chance of doing. Having thus settled accounts with my readers; I take up again the thread of my story, and thus I proceed.

Mr. Hartley being now, as he believed, upon the point of disposing of his daughter in marriage, began seriously to consider that he should want a female companion to manage, his family, to nurse his ailments, and to repair the breaches, that the hand of wintry time had made in his spirits and his constitution. The reader will be pleased to recollect, that he had already laid siege to the heart of the gentle Sophia. He now prosecuted his affair with more alacrity than ever.

Alas, my dear readers! while we have been junketting along from Southampton to Oxford, from Oxford to Windsor, and from Windsor to Southampton back again, such is the miserable fate of human kind! Miss Amelia Wilhelmina Cranley, the most pious of her sex, the flower of Mr. Whitfield's converts, the wonder and admiration of Roger the cobler, has given up the ghost. You will please then, in what follows, to represent to yourselves the charms of Sophia as decked and burnished with a suit of sables. Her exterior indeed was sable and gloomy, but her heart was far superior to the attacks of wayward fate. She sat aloft in the region of philosophy. She steeled her heart with the dignity of republicanism; for her to drop one tear of sorrow would have been an eternal disgrace.

About this time--it was perhaps in reality a manoeuvre to forward the affair, to which she had no aversion at bottom, with the father of Delia--that Miss Cranley gave a grand entertainment, at which were present Mr. Hartley, Mr. Prattle, sir William Twyford, lord Martin, most of the ladies we have already commemorated, and many others.

The repast was conducted with much solemnity. The masculine character of the mind of Sophia had rendered her particularly attached to the grace of action.

When she drank the health of any of her guests, she accompanied it with a most profound *conge*. When she invited them to partake of any dish, she pointed towards it with her hand. This action might have served to display a graceful arm, but, alas! upon hers the hand of time had been making depredations, and it appeared somewhat coarse and discoloured.

After dinner, the lady of the house, as usual, turned the conversation upon the subject of politics. She inveighed with much warmth against the effeminacy and depravity of the modern times. We were slaves, and we deserved to be so. In almost every country there now appeared a king, that puppet pageant, that monster in creation, miserable itself, a combination of every vice, and invented for the curse of human kind. "Where now," she asked, "was the sternness and inflexibility of ancient story? Where was that Junius, that stood and gazed in triumph upon the execution of his sons? Where that Fabricius, that turned up his nose under the snout of an elephant? Where was that Marcus Brutus, who sent his dagger to the heart of Caesar? For her part, she believed, and she would not give the snap of her fingers for him if it were otherwise, that he was in reality, as sage historians have reported, the son of Julius."

In the very paroxysm of her oratory she chanced to cast her eyes upon Mr. Prattle. With the character of Mr. Prattle, the reader is already partly acquainted. But he does not yet know, for it was not necessary for our story he should do so, that the honourable Mr. Prattle was a commoner and a placeman. Good God, sir, represent to yourself with what a flame of indignation our amazon surveyed him! She rose from her seat, and, taking him by the hand, very familiarly turned him round in the middle of the company. "This," said she, "is one of our Fabiuses, one of our Decii. Good God, my friend, what would you do, if a brother officer shook a cane over your shoulders as he did over those of the divine Themistocles? What would you do, if the brutal lull of an Appius ravished from your arms an only daughter? But I beg your pardon, sir. You are a placeman, mutually disgracing and disgraced. You sell your constituents to the vilest ministers, that ever came forward the champions of despotism. And those ministers show us what is their insignificance, their impotence, their want of discernment, in giving such a thing as you are, places of so great importance, offices of so high emolument."

Mr. Prattle, unused to be treated so cavalierly, and arraigned before so large a company, trembled in every limb: "My dear madam, my sweet Miss Sophia, pray do not pinch quite so hard;" and the water stood in his eyes. Unable however to elude her grasp he fell down upon his knees. "For God's sake! Oh dear! Oh lack a daisy! Why, Miss, sure you are mad." Miss Cranley, unheedful of his exclamations, was however just going to begin with more vehemence than ever, when a sudden accident put a stop to the torrent of her oratory. But this event cannot be properly related without going back a little in our narrative, and acquainting the reader with some of those circumstances by which it was produced.

CHAPTER VI.

A Catastrophe.

Sir William Twyford had gained great credit with lord Martin by his conduct in the affair of Mr. Prettyman. He now imagined that he saw an opening for the exercise of his humour, which he was never able to refill. He communicated his plan to lord Martin. By his assistance he procured that implement, which school-boys have denominated a cracker. This his lordship found an opportunity of attaching to the skirt of Miss Cranley's sack. At the moment we have described, when she was again going to enter into the stream of her rhetoric, which, great as it naturally was, was now somewhat improved with copious draughts of claret, the cracker was set on fire.

Poor Sophia now started in great agitation. "Bounce, bounce," went the cracker. Sophia skipped and danced from one end of the room to the other. "Great gods of Rome," exclaimed she, "Jupiter, Minerva, and all the celestial and infernal deities!" The force of the cracker was now somewhat spent. "Ye boys of Britain, that bear not one mark of manhood about you! Would Leonidas have fastened a squib to the robe of the Spartan mother? Would Cimber have so unworthily used Portia, the wife of Brutus? Would Corbulo thus have interrupted the heroic fortitude of Arria, the spouse of Thrasea Paetus?"

"My dear madam," exclaimed lord Martin, his eyes glistening with triumph, "with all submission, Corbulo I believe had been assassinated, before Arria so gloriously put an end to her existence." "Thou thing," cried Miss Cranky, "and hast thou escaped the torrent of my invective! Thou eternal blot to the list, in which are inserted the names of a Faulkland, a Shaftesbury, a Somers, and above all, that Leicester, who so bravely threw the lie in the face of his sovereign!" "He! he!" cried lord Martin, who could no longer refrain from boasting of his great atchievement. If I have escaped your vengeance, let me tell you, madam, you have not escaped "mine." "And was it thee, thou nincompoop? Hence, thou wretch! Avaunt! Begone, or thou shalt feel my fury!" Saying this, she clenched her fist, and closed her teeth, with so threatening an aspect, that the little peer was very much terrified. He flew back several paces. "My dear Miss Griskin," said he, "protect me! This barbarous woman does not understand wit,"--and he precipitately burst out of the room. The lady too was so much discomposed, that she thought proper to retire, assuring the company that she would attend them again in a moment.

"Well," cried Miss Griskin, as soon as she had disappeared, "this was the nicest fun!" "I was afraid," said Miss Prim, "it would have discomposed Miss Cranley's petticoats." "Law, my dear!" said Miss Gawky, "by my so, I like the music of a cracker, better than all the concerts in the varsal world." We need not inform our readers, that Miss Languish, in the very height and altitude of the confusion, had been obliged to retire.

Lord Martin, in the midst of his triumph and exultation, had not leisure to recollect, nor perhaps penetration to perceive, the effect that this little sally might have upon his interests. Despotic and boorish as was the genius of Mr. Hartley, it cowred under that of Sophia with the most abject servility. And that lady now vowed eternal war against the heroical peer.

"Mr. Hartley," said she, in their next *tete a tete*, "let me tell you, lord Martin, must never have Miss Delia." "My dearest life," said the old gentleman, "consider, the day is fixed, my word is passed, and it is too late to revoke now. Beside, lord Martin has ten thousand pounds a year." "Ten thousand figs," said she, "do not tell me, it is never too late to be wife. Lord Martin is a venal senator, and a little sniveling fellow." "My dear," said Hartley, "I never differed from you before: do let me have my mind now." "Have your mind, sir! Men should have no minds. Tyrants that they are! And now I think of it, Miss Delia does not like lord Martin." "Pooh," said Mr. Hartley, recovering spirit at such an objection, "that is all stuff and nonsense." "Nonsense! Let me tell you, sir, women are not ***born to be controled***. They are queens of the creation, and if they had their way, and the government of the world was in their hands, things would go much better than they do." "I know they would," replied her admirer, "if they were all as wise as you." "Child," returned Sophia, turning up her nose, "that is neither here nor there. The matter in short is this. Damon loves Delia, and Delia loves Damon. And if your daughter be not Mrs. Villiers, I will never be Mrs. Hartley."

From a decision like this there could be no appeal. Mr. Hartley told lord Martin, the next time he came to his house to pay his devoirs to his mistress, that he had altered his mind. His lordship was too much surprised at this manoeuvre to make any immediate answer; so turned upon his heel, and decamped.

The happy revolution, by the intervention of Miss Fletcher, was soon made known to sir William and his friend. Damon now paid his addresses in form. A reconciliation took place between Mr. Moreland and the father of our heroine. The marriage was publicly talked of, the day was fixed, and every thing prepared for the nuptials.

It is impossible to describe the happiness of our lovers, when they saw every obstacle thus unexpectedly removed. Damon was beside himself with surprise and congratulation. Delia, at intervals, rubbed her eyes, and could scarcely be persuaded that it was not a dream. They saw each other at least once every day. Together they wandered along the margin of the ocean, and together they sought that delicious alcove, which now appeared ten times more beautiful, from the recollection it suggested of the sufferings they had passed.

Lord Martin was in the mean time most grievously disappointed. "The devil damn the fellow!" said he, "he crosses me like my evil genius. I have a month's mind to send him a challenge. He is a tall, big looking fellow to be sure. But then if I could contrive to kill him. Ah, me! but fortune does not always favour the brave. My reputation is established. I do not want a duel for that. And for any other purpose, it is all a lottery. Fire and furies, death and destruction! something must be done. Let me think--*About my brain*."

But lord Martin was not the only one whose hopes were disappointed, by the expected marriage of Delia. He loved her not, he felt not one flutter of complacency about his heart. It was vanity that first prompted him to address her. It was disappointed pride that now stung him. Even Mr. Prattle viewed her with a more generous affection. His genius was not indeed a daring one, but it was active and indefatigable. Squire Savage did not feel the less, though he did not spend many words about it. He was a blustering hector. He had the reputation of fearing nothing, and caring for nothing, that stood in his way. There were also other lovers beside these, ***whom the muse knows not, nor desires to know***.

In this manner gins and snares seemed, on every side, to surround our happy and heedless lovers. They sported on the brink. They sighed, and smiled, and sang, and talked again. At length the eve of the day, from which their future happiness was to be dated, arrived. They had but one drawback, the continued averseness of lord Thomas Villiers. Damon was however now obliged, together with Mr. Hartley, to attend the lawyers at Mr. Moreland's, in order to complete the previous formalities.

CHAPTER VII.
Containing what will terrify the reader.

At such a moment as this, a mind of delicacy and sensibility is fond of solitude. Delia told Mrs. Bridget, that she would take her usual walk, and be home time enough to superintend the oeconomy of supper, at which the company of Damon and sir William Twyford was expected.

They accordingly arrived before nine o'clock. Mrs. Bridget expected her mistress every moment. Damon and his friend would have gone out to meet her, but they were not willing to leave Mr. Hartley alone. The clock however struck ten, and no Delia appeared. Every one now began to be seriously uneasy. Damon and sir William went in both her most favourite walks to find her, but in vain. Messengers were dispatched twenty different ways. The lover repaired to the mansion of Lord Martin. The baronet immediately set out for the house of Mr. Savage.

Mr. Hartley, who, with the external of a bear, and the heart of a miser, was not destitute of the feelings of a parent, was now exceedingly agitated. He strided up and down the room with incredible velocity. He bit his fingers with anxiety, and threw his wig into the fire. "As I am a good man," said he, "Mr. Prattle lives but almost next door, and I will go to him." Mr. Prattle was at home, and having heard his story, condoled with him upon it with much apparent sincerity.

Damon met with the same success. Lord Martin received him with perfect serenity. "Bless us," cried he, "and is Miss Delia gone? I never was more astonished in my life. I do not know what to do," and he took a pinch of snuff. "Mr. Villiers," said he, with the utmost gravity, "I have all possible respect for you. Blast me! if I am not willing to forget all our former rivalship. Tell me, sir, can I do you any service?" Damon had every reason to be satisfied with his behaviour, and flew out of the house in a moment.

Sir William Twyford did not however meet with the person he went in quest of. Miss Savage informed him, that her brother, not two hours ago, had received a letter, and immediately, without informing her of his design, which indeed he very seldom did, ordered his best hunter out of the stable. She added, that she had imagined, that he had received a summons to a fox-chace early the next morning.

Such was the account brought by sir William to the anxious and distracted Damon. "Alas," cried he, "it is but too plain? She is by this time in the hands of that insensible boor. Oh, who can bear to think of it! He is perhaps, at this moment, tormenting her with his nauseous familiarities, and griping her soft and tender limbs! Oh, why was I born! Why was I ever cheated with the phantom of happiness! Wretch, wretch that I am!"

With these words he burst out of the house, and flew along with surprising rapidity. Sir William, having hastily ordered everything to be prepared for a pursuit, immediately followed him. He found him, wafted, spent, and almost insensible, lying beside a little brook that crossed the road. The baronet raised him in his arms, and, with the gentlest accents that friendship ever poured into a mortal ear, recovered him to life and perception.

"Where am I?" said the disconsolate lover. "Who are you? ah, my friend, my best, my tried friend! I know you now. How came I here? Has any thing unfortunate happened? Where is my Delia?" "Let us seek her, my Villiers," said the baronet. "Seek her! What! is she lost? Oh, yes, I recollect it now; she is gone, snatched from my arms. Let us pursue her! Let us overtake her Oh that it may not be too late."

He now leaned upon the shoulder of his friend, and returned with painful and irregular steps. His disorder was so great, that sir William thought it best to have him immediately conveyed to a chamber. He was so much exhausted, that this was easily accomplished, without his being perfectly sensible what was done. The baronet, with three servants mounted on horseback, immediately pursued the road towards London.--Having thus related the confusion and grief that were occasioned by her sudden disappearance, we will now return to our heroine.

She had advanced, according to the intention she had hinted to her servant, towards the grove, where she had so often wandered with her beloved. She was wrapped up and lost in the contemplation of her approaching felicity. "And is every difficulty surmounted, and shall at last my fate be twined with Damon's? Sure, it is too much, it cannot be! Fate does not deal so partially with mortals. To bestow so vast a happiness on one, while thousands pine in helpless misery. But let me not be incredulous. Let me not be ungrateful. No, since heaven has thus accumulated its favours on me, my future days shall all be spent in raising the oppressed, and cheering the disconsolate. I will remember that I also have tasted the cup of woe, that I have looked forward to disappointment and despair. ***Taught by the hand that pities me,*** I will learn to pity others."

She was thus musing with herself, she was thus full of piety and virtuous resolution, when, on a sudden, a trampling of horses behind her, roused her from her reverie. Two persons advanced. But before she had time to examine their features, or even to remove out of the path, by which they seemed to be coming, the foremost of them leaping hastily upon the ground, seized her by the waist, arid, in spite of all her struggling, placed her on the front of the saddle, and instantly mounted with the utmost agility. Cries and tears were vain. They were in a solitary path, little beaten by the careful husbandman, or the gay votaries of fashion. She was now hurried along, and generally at full speed, through a thousand bye paths, that seemed capable of puzzling the most assiduous pursuit.

They had scarcely advanced two little miles, ere they arrived at a large and broad highway. Here they found a chariot ready waiting for them, into which Delia was immediately thrust. She now for the first time lifted up her eyes. The first object to which she attended was the faces of her ravishers. Of him who had been the most active, she had not the smallest recollection. The other who was in a livery, she imagined she had seen somewhere, though, in the present confusion of her mind, she could not fix upon the place. She next looked round her with wildness and eagerness, as far as her eye could reach, to see if there were no protector, no deliverance near. But she looked in vain. All was solitude and stilness. The murmurs, the activity of the day were past. And now, the silver moon in radiant majesty shed a solemn serenity ever the whole scene. Serenity, alas! to the heart at ease, but nothing could bring serenity to the troubled breast of Delia.

As her last resource, she appealed to those who by brutal force had carried her away. "Oh, if you have any hearts, any thing human that dwells about you, pity a poor, forlorn, and helpless maid! Alas, in what have I injured you? What would you do to me?" "Oh, pray, Miss, do not be frightened," said the first ravisher with an accent of familiar vulgarity, "we will do you no harm, we mean nothing but your good. You will make your fortune. You never had such luck in your life. You will have reason to thank us the longest day you can ever know."

CHAPTER VIII.

A Denouement.

At this moment, Delia with infinite transport, heard the sound of horses at a distance. Every thing was quiet. Our heroine listened with eager expectation, and those who guarded her looked out to see who it was that approached. Suspense was not long on either side. The horsemen were up with them in a moment. "Oh, whoever you are," cried Delia, in an agony of distress, "pity and relieve the most miserable woman"----She received no answer, but the horses stopped, and lord Martin was in a moment at the door of the carriage. "Oh, my lord," cried Delia, "is it you? Thanks, eternal thanks, for this fortunate incident. If you had not come, heaven knows what would have become of me! Those brutes, those wretches--But conduct me, my lord, to my father's house. Without doubt, they must by this time be in a terrible fright."

"Do not be uneasy," cried his lordship, endeavouring to assume an harmonious, but missing his point, he spoke in the shrillest and most squeaking accent that can be imagined. "Do not be uneasy, my charmer. You are in the hands of a man, that loves you, as never woman was loved before. But I will be with you in a minute," said he. And withdrawing behind the carriage, he beckoned to the person who had conducted the business of the rape. "Why, you incorrigible blockhead," said lord

Martin, "you have neglected half your instructions. Why, her hands are at liberty." "I beg your honour's pardon," replied the pimp, "I had indeed forgotten, but it shall be remedied in a moment." And saying this, he pulled a strong ribband out of his pocket, and getting into the chariot, fastened the soft and lily hands of our heroine behind her. She screamed, and invoked the name of his lordship a thousand times. Her hair became disentangled from its ligaments, and flowed in waving ringlets about her snowy, panting bosom. Exhausted with continual agitation, and particularly with the last struggle, she seemed ready to faint, but was quickly restored by the assiduity of these sordid grooms.

Before she had completely recovered her recollection, lord Martin had seated himself in the carriage, and was drawing up some of the blinds. "Drive on," said he to the coachman, who was by this time mounted into the box, "Drive, as if the devil was behind you." The cavalcade accordingly went forward. There was a servant on each side of the carriage, beside the commander in chief, who occasionally advanced in the front, and occasionally brought up the rear.

"And whither," said the affrighted Delia, "whither are we going? This cannot be the way to Southampton. What do you mean? But ah, it is too plain! Why else this impotence of insult?" endeavouring to disengage her hands. And she turned from him in a rage of indignation. "Ah," cried his lordship, "do not avert those brilliant eyes! Turn them towards me, and they will outshine the lustre of the morn, and I shall perceive nothing of the sun, even when he gains his meridian height." "And thou despicable wretch, is this thy shallow plan? And what dost thou think to do with me? Mountains shall sooner bend their lofty summits to the earth, than I will ever waste a thought on thee." "Do with thee, my fairest!" cried the peer, "why, marry thee. Dost thou think that the paltry Damon shall get the better of my eagle genius? No. Fortune now unfurls my standard, and I drive the *frighted fates* before me." "Boastful, empty coward! Thou darest not even brave a woman's rage. If my hands were at liberty, I would tear out those insolent eyes." "*Go on*, thou gentlest of thy sex, *and charm me with that angel voice*! For though thou dealest in threats, abuse, and proud defiance, *it is heaven to hear thee*."

Such was the courtship that passed between our heroine and her triumphant admirer. They had new proceeded twenty miles, and the midnight bell had tolled near half an hour. They had passed through one turnpike, and Delia had endeavoured by cries and prayers to obtain some assistance. But the person who opened to them was alone, and though ever so desirous, could not have resisted such a cavalcade. Beside this, the pimp told him a plausible story of a wanton wife, and an injured husband, with the particulars of which we do not think it necessary to trouble our readers. They had also seen one foot passenger, and two horsemen. But they were eluded and amused by a repetition of the same stratagem.

Delia, having exhausted her first rage and astonishment, had now remained for some time silent. She revolved in her mind all the particulars of her situation. She had at first considered her ravisher in no other light than as hateful and despicable, but she was now compelled to regard this venomous little animal, as the arbiter of her fate, and the master of her fortunes. She reflected with horror, how much she was in his power, what ill usage he might inflict, and to what extremities he might reduce her. She now seriously thought of exerting herself to melt him into pity, and to persuade him, by every argument she could invent, to spare and to release her. "Ah, where," thought she, "is my Damon? Why does not he appear to succour me? Alas, what distresses, what agonies may he not even now endure!"

Full of these, and a thousand other tormenting reflections, she burst into a flood of tears. Lord Martin drew from his pocket a clean cambric handkerchief, and, carefully unfolding it, wiped away the drops as they fell. "Loveliest of creatures," said he, "by the murmuring of thy voice, the heaving of thy bosom, the distraction of thy looks, and by these tears, I should imagine thou wert uneasy." "Ah," cried Delia unheedful of his words, "what shall I say to move him?" "Oh, talk for ever," replied his lordship. "The winds shall forget to whistle, and the seas to roar. Noisy mobs shall cease their huzzas, and the din of war be still; for there is music in thy voice." "Oh," exclaimed our heroine, "let one touch of compassion approach thy soul. Indeed, my lord, I can never have you. Release me, and I will forgive what is past, and Damon shall never notice it." "Zounds and fire!" cried the peer, "dost thou think to prevail with me by the motives of a coward? But why dost thou talk of Damon? Look on me. Behold this purple coat, and fine *toupee*. Think on my estate, and think on my title."

But at this moment the oratory of his lordship ceased to be heard. At a small distance there appeared two persons, the one on foot, and whose air, so far as it could be perceived by the imperfect light, was genteel, and the other on horseback, engaged in earnest conference. As the carriage drew towards them, Delia exclaimed, in a piercing, but pathetic voice, "Help! help! for God's sake! Rape! Murder! Help!" The voice immediately caught the young gentleman on foot, who approached the carriage.--But before we proceed any farther we will inform our readers who these persons were.

The gentleman on foot, was Mr. Godfrey. He was on a visit to a sister, who lived very near the spot upon which he now stood. She was married to a substantial yeoman, who rented an estate in this place, the property of lord Thomas Villiers. The beautiful scenes of nature were particularly congenial to the elegant said contemplative mind of Mr. Godfrey. And he had now, as was frequently his custom, strolled out to enjoy the calm serenity, and the splendid beauty, of a midnight scene. The man on horse-back was a thief taker, who, just before the carriage had driven up, had, without ceremony, accosted Mr. Godfrey with his enquiries, and a description of the person of whom he was in pursuit.

CHAPTER IX.
Which dismisses the Reader.

Mr. Godfrey, in a resolute tone, called out to the coachman to stop, and not contented with a verbal mandate, he rushed before the horses, and brandishing a club he held in his hand, bid the driver proceed at his peril. "Drive on," said lord Martin, thrusting his head out at the window--"Drive on, and be damned to you!" At this moment the pimp rode up. "It is nothing," said he, "but a poor gentleman, who has just forced his wife from the arms of a gallant." "Oh no!" cried Delia. "I am not his wife. I am an innocent woman, whom he has forced from her father and her lover."

The thief taker out of curiosity rode forward. "That," said he, fixing his eye upon the pimp, "that is the very rascal I am in search of." The pimp, who had only been borrowed by lord Martin of one of his more experienced acquaintance, no sooner heard the sound, than, accounting for it with infinite facility and readiness of mind, he turned about his horse, and attempted to fly. One of the footmen, naturally a coward, and terrified at these incidents, with the meaning of which he was unacquainted, imitated his example. The other came forward to the assistance of his master, and was laid prostrate upon the ground, by Mr. Godfrey with one blow. The thief taker had the start of the pimp, and overtook him in a moment.

Mr. Godfrey now opened the door of the carriage. But the little peer was prepared for this incident, and having his sword drawn, made a sudden pass at our generous knight-errant. The latter, with infinite agility, leaped aside, and lifting up his club, shivered the sword into a thousand pieces.

"Death and the devil! Pox confound you!" said lord Martin, and endeavoured to draw a pistol from his pocket. But the unsuccessful pass he had made had thrown him somewhat off his bias, and though he had employed more than one effort, he had not been able to recover himself. At this instant, Mr. Godfrey seized him by the collar, and with a sudden-whirl, threw him into the middle of the road. "Fire and"--his lordship had not time to finish his exclamation. The part of the road in which he fell was exceeding dirty. The workmen had been employed the preceding day, in scraping the mud together into a heap against the bank, and his lordship, unable to overcome the velocity with which he trundled along, rolled into the midst of it in an instant. He was entirely lost in this soft receptacle. The colour of his purple coat, and his lily white **toupee**, could no longer be distinguished.

The coachman, perceiving the disaster of his lord, now leaped from the box. Mr. Godfrey had scarcely had time to reduce this new antagonist to a state of inactivity, before the footman, upon whom he had first displayed his prowess, began to discover some signs of life. He might have been yet overpowered in spite of all his valour and presence of mind, if the house of his brother-in-law, had not fortunately been so near, that the shrieks of Delia, and the altercation of her ravishers reached it. The honest farmer was at the window in a moment, and perceiving that his brother was engaged in the affray, he huddled on his clothes with all expedition, and now appeared in the highway.

The victory was immediately decided. The footman perceiving this new reinforcement, did not dare to act upon the offensive, and Mr. Godfrey mounted into the chariot to assist our heroine. He now first perceived that her hands were manacled. From this restraint however, he suddenly disengaged her, and taking her in his arms out of the carriage, he delivered her to his sister, who advanced at this moment.

The footman, assisted by the humanity of the farmer, was now employed in raising his master. His lordship made the most pitiable figure that can be imagined. His features, as well as his dress, wore an appearance perfectly uniform. "Whither would you convey him?" said Mr. Godfrey, who was now returned. "What shall we do with him?" "Oh, and please you, sir," said the footman, "his lordship has a house about half a mile off." Lord Martin now first discovered some marks of sensibility, and ***shook his goary locks***. "His lordship!" exclaimed the yeoman. "Sure it cannot be--yet it is--by my soul I cannot tell whether it be lord Martin or no." The coachman now rose from the ground, and began with a profound bow to his master. "And please your honour," said he, "we have made a sad day's work of it. Your worship makes but a pitiful figure. Faugh! I think as how, if I dared say so much, begging your honour's pardon, that your lordship stinks." "Put him into the carriage," cried Mr. Godfrey, "and drive him home." Lord Martin, now first recovered his tongue, and wiping away the mud from his eyes, "And so it was you, sir, I suppose," cried he, "to whom I am obliged for this catastrophe. But pox take me, if you shall not hear of it. Ten thousand curses on my wayward fate! The devil take it! Death and damnation!" During this soliloquy, the servants were employed in placing their lord in the chariot. The coachman mounted the box, and by this time they were out of hearing.

Mr. Godfrey and his brother now entered the house. Delia was seated in a chair, her hair dishevelled, her features disordered, and her dress in the most bewitching confusion. But how much were both the deliverer and the heroine surprised, when they mutually recognised each others features! Mr. Godfrey made Delia a very polite compliment upon her escape, and congratulated himself, in the warmest language, for having been the fortunate instrument.

They now retired to rest. The next morning, Delia was much better recovered from her terror and fatigue, than could have been expected. Mr. Godfrey however had not thought it adviseable that she should be removed that day, and had therefore set off early in the morning for Southampton, that he might himself be the messenger of these happy tidings.

"I hope Miss," said Mrs. Wilson, who attended our heroine, "that you will dress yourself as well as you can." "And why" cried Delia, "do you desire that? I can see nobody, I can think of nothing, but my absent and anxious Damon." "Let us hope," replied the other, "that he is very well. But, Miss, we expect lord Thomas Villiers by dinner time." "Lord Thomas Villiers!" exclaimed Delia, in the extremest surprise. "Yes," cried Mrs. Wilson. "He is our landlord, and he always comes over once about this time of the year." "Alas," said Delia, "I can see nobody. But I had rather meet any person at this time, than lord Thomas Villiers." "Bless me, Miss! why I am sure he is a very good sort of a gentleman." "I dare say he is," cried Delia. "But indeed, and indeed, Mrs. Wilson, I cannot see him. Pray oblige me in this." "Law, well I cannot think what objection you can have! There must be something very particular in it."

Such were the hints that Mrs. Wilson threw out for the satisfying of her curiosity, but Delia was not disposed to be more communicative. The good woman however, with the error of our heroine before her eyes, was determined not to commit a similar fault. Lord Thomas was therefore scarcely arrived, before she set open the flood gates of her eloquence, in describing the rescue, and the unrivalled beauty of the lady under her roof.

His lordship had long had a misunderstanding with lord Martin upon the subject of their contiguous estates. As his temper was not the most gentle, nor his memory upon these subjects the most treacherous, he expressed his triumph in loud shouts, and repeated horse laughs, upon the recent defeat of his antagonist. Nothing however would content him but a sight of the lady. "That," said Mrs. Wilson, "my guess is too nice to consent to. You must know, she has a particular dislike to your lordship." "A dislike to me!" said the old gentleman, whose curiosity was now more inflamed than even "Will you be contented," said his kind hostess, "with a peep through the key hole!" and without waiting for an answer, she took him by the hand, and led him up stairs. "By my foul!" said his lordship, "she is the finest woman in the world. Devil take me, if I can contain myself," and he burst into the room.

Lord Thomas advanced a few steps, and then stopping, clasped his hands; "Why she is an angel of a woman! And did Martin, that dirty scoundrel, think he could run away with you? Impudent, pot-bellied spider! Ah, if my son had fallen in love with such a woman as you, I could forgive him any thing." And seizing her hand he pressed it to his lips. "Forgive me, charmer," cried he, "I am an old fellow. I will do you no harm."

Delia, though pleased with the behaviour of her intended father-in-law, dared not yet discover herself to him. In the afternoon, Mr. Godfrey, and Sir William Twyford, arrived. Damon, agitated as he was by the most dreadful images that a troubled fancy could suggest, appeared in the morning in a high fever. Instead of being able to hasten to the mistress of his soul, he was confined to his bed, and attended by physicians.

"Ha," cried lord Thomas, as soon as he saw the baronet, "and who sent for you? What do you want? I think, Sir, you are the gentleman to whom I am obliged for telling my son, that duty to parents is a baby prejudice, that obstinacy is a heroic virtue, and that fortune, fame, and friends, are all to be sacrificed to the whining passion, which, I think, you call love." "My lord," replied the baronet, "I have done nothing, of which I feel any reason to be ashamed. But a subject more pressing calls for my immediate attention." Then turning to Delia, "Give me leave to congratulate you, madam, and heaven can tell how heartily I do it, upon the generous and happy interposition of Mr. Godfrey." "And pray," interrupted lord Thomas, "how came you acquainted with that lady?" "Oh, tell me," cried Delia, with an impatience not to be restrained by modes and forms, "tell me, how does my Damon? Why is he not here? Alas, I fear"--"Fear nothing," cried the baronet. "He is safe. He is at your father's house, and impatient to see you." "And is this the lady," cried lord Thomas, "of whom my son is enamoured? But he shall not disobey me. I will never permit it. Sir, if this be the lady, I will give her to him with my own hand. But where is the ungracious rascal? Why does not he appear?" "Nothing, be assured," said the baronet, "but reasons of the last importance, could have kept him back in so interesting a moment." "Alas, I fear," cried Delia, "since you endeavour to conceal them from me, they are reasons of the most afflicting nature." "It is in vain," replied Sir William, "to endeavour at concealment." "Your son," turning to lord Thomas Villiers, "is confined to his bed. The anxiety and fatigue that he suffered, in consequence of the extraordinary step of lord Martin, have thrown him into a fever. But be not uneasy, my Delia," taking her hand, "there is no danger. One sigh, one look from you will restore him." "Ten thousand curses," exclaimed the father, "upon the head of the contemptible, misbegotten ravisher! But let us make haste. I am glad however that my rogue of a son is a little punished for his impertinence. Let us make haste."

Saying this, he ordered the horses to his chariot, and the whole company prepared to set out for Southampton immediately. The only business which remained, was the dispatching a message, which was done by one of sir William's servants, from Mr. Godfrey to lord Martin, announcing his name, and informing his lordship, that he was to be met with any time in the ensuing week at Mr. Moreland's.

Lord Martin was a good deal bruised and enfeebled with the adventure of the preceding evening. He had been obliged to undergo a lustration of near an hour, before he could be put to bed. He was just risen, when the message was delivered. "Zounds!" cried the peer, "he is, is he? And so this fellow, whom nobody knows, has the impudence to snub me! By my title, and all the blood of my ancestors, he is not worthy of my sword. I will have him assassinated. I will hire some blackguards to seize him, and bind him in my presence, and I will bastinado him with my own hand. Furies and curses! I do not know what to do. Oh, this confounded vanity! Not contented with one disgrace, I have brought upon myself another, ten times more mortifying than the first. By Tartarus, and all the infernal gods, I believe I had better let it rest where it is! Wretch, wretch, that I am!" And he threw himself on the bed in an agony of despair.

Damon had slept little the preceding night, and his slumbers had been disturbed with a thousand horrible imaginations. The first person who appeared in his chamber the next morning he addressed with "Where, where is she? Where is my Delia? My life, my soul, the mistress of my fate? Ah, why do you look so haggard, so unconsoling. You have heard nothing of her? Give me my clothes. I will pursue her to the world's end. I will find her, though she be hid deep as the centre." "Sir, be pacified," said the servant, "she is safe." "Safe," cried our lover, "why then does she not appear to comfort me? But haste, I will fly to her. I will clasp, I will lock her, in my arms. No, nothing, not all the powers on earth, shall ever part us more." "Sir, she is not in the house." "Not in the house," cried Damon starting, "Ha! say. I will not be cheated. On thy life do not trifle with my impatience."

At this moment Mr. Godfrey entered the room. "Who is there?" cried Damon, starting at every whisper. "It is your friend," said Godfrey. "A friend that owes you much, and would willingly pay you something back again." "I do not understand you," replied our hero. "I can talk of nothing but my Delia. Oh Delia! Delia! I will teach thy name to all the echoes. I will send it with every wind to heaven. Ever, ever, shall it dwell upon my lips." "Delia," replied the other, "is in safety. I have been so happy as to rescue her." "Ha! sayest thou? let me look upon thee well. I am somewhat disordered, but I think thy name is Godfrey. Thou shouldst not deceive me. Thou art not old in falsehood." "I do not deceive thee. On my life I do not!" exclaimed Godfrey, with emotion. "Compose thyself for a few hours. Or ever thou shalt see the setting sun, I will put thy Delia into thy arms again."

Damon was somewhat composed by these assurances. No voice like that of Godfrey had power to sooth his mind to serenity. But though he sought to restrain himself, he listened to every noise. He started at the sound of every foot, and the rattle of a carriage in the street agitated his soul almost to frenzy.

"Why does not she come? What can delay her? I have counted every moment. I have waited whole ages. I see, I see, that every thing conspires to cheat, and to distract me. Damon has not one friend left to whisper in his ear--to whisper what? That Delia is no more? That all her beauties are defaced, by some sacrilegious hand? That all her heaven of charms have been rifled? Oh, no. I must not think of that. But hark! I thought I heard a sound, but it is delirium all. Sure, sure it comes this way. I will listen but this once."

The door of the chamber now flew open. But oh, what object caught the raptured eye of Damon! He was just risen. "It is, it is my Delia!" and they flew into each others arms. But having embraced for a moment, Damon took hold of her hand, and held her from him. "Let me look at thee. And is it Delia? And art thou safe, unhurt? I would not be mistaken." "Yes, I am she, and ten times more my Damon's than ever." "It is enough. I am contented. But hark! who comes there? Sure it is not the brutal ravisher? No," cried he, in a voice of surprise, "it is my father."

Lord Thomas Villiers, who had been a witness of this scene, could restrain himself no longer. "Come to my arms, thy father's arms," cried he, "and let me bless thee." "Stay, stay," cried Damon. "Yes I know thee well. But I will never be separated from her any more. I will laugh at the authority of a parent. Tyranny and tortures shall not rend me from her." "The authority of a parent," replied lord Thomas, "shall never more be employed to counteract thy wishes. I myself will join your hands."

The constitution of Damon was so full of sensibility, that it was some days before he was completely recovered. In the mean time, the amours of Sir William Twyford, and Mr. Hartley, continually ripened, and it was proposed, that the three parties should be united in the same day.

"And now," said Damon, "I have but one care more, one additional exertion, to set my mind at ease. My Godfrey, I owe thee more than kingdoms can repay. Tell me, instruct me, what can I do to serve you? Damon must be the most contemptible of villains, if he could think his felicity complete, when his Godfrey was unhappy."

"Think not of me," said Godfrey, "I am happy in the way that nature intended, beyond even the power of Damon to make me. Since I saw you, a favourable change has taken place in my circumstances. In spite of various obstacles, I have brought a tragedy upon the stage, and it has met with distinguished success. My former crosses and mortifications are all forgotten. Philosophers may tell us, that reputation, and the immortality of a name, are all but an airy shadow. Enough for me, that nature, from my earliest infancy, led me to place my first delight in these. I envy not kings their sceptres. I envy not statesmen their power. I envy not Damon his love, and his Delia. Next to the pursuits of honour and truth, my soul is conscious to but one wish, that of having my name enrolled, in however inferior a rank, with a Homer, and a Horace, a Livy, and a Cicero."

The next day the proposed weddings took place. It is natural perhaps, at the conclusion of such a narrative as this, to represent them all as happy. But we are bound to adhere to nature and truth. Mr. Hartley and his politician for some time struggled for superiority, but, in the end, the eagle genius of Sophia soared aloft. Sir William, though he married a woman, good natured, and destitute of vice, found something more insipid in marriage, than he had previously apprehended. For Damon and his Delia, they were amiable, and constant. Though their hearts were in the highest degree susceptible and affectionate, the first ebullition of passion could not last for ever. But it was succeeded by *the feast of reason, and the flow of soul*. Their hours were sped with the calmness of tranquility. When they saw each other no longer with transport, they saw each other with complacency. And so long as they live, they will doubtless afford the most striking demonstration, that marriage, when it unites two gentle souls, and meaned by nature for each other, when it is blest of heaven, and accompanied with reason and discretion, is the sweetest, and the fairest of all the bands of society.

THE END.

The Codes Of Hammurabi And Moses
W. W. Davies

QTY

The discovery of the Hammurabi Code is one of the greatest achievements of archaeology, and is of paramount interest, not only to the student of the Bible, but also to all those interested in ancient history...

Religion ISBN: *1-59462-338-4*

Pages:132
MSRP $12.95

The Theory of Moral Sentiments
Adam Smith

QTY

This work from 1749. contains original theories of conscience amd moral judgment and it is the foundation for systemof morals.

Philosophy ISBN: *1-59462-777-0*

Pages:536
MSRP $19.95

Jessica's First Prayer
Hesba Stretton

QTY

In a screened and secluded corner of one of the many railway-bridges which span the streets of London there could be seen a few years ago, from five o'clock every morning until half past eight, a tidily set-out coffee-stall, consisting of a trestle and board, upon which stood two large tin cans, with a small fire of charcoal burning under each so as to keep the coffee boiling during the early hours of the morning when the work-people were thronging into the city on their way to their daily toil...

Pages:84

Childrens ISBN: *1-59462-373-2*

MSRP $9.95

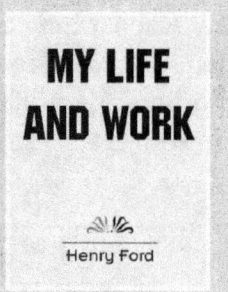

My Life and Work
Henry Ford

QTY

Henry Ford revolutionized the world with his implementation of mass production for the Model T automobile. Gain valuable business insight into his life and work with his own auto-biography... "We have only started on our development of our country we have not as yet, with all our talk of wonderful progress, done more than scratch the surface. The progress has been wonderful enough but..."

Pages:300

Biographies/ ISBN: *1-59462-198-5*

MSRP $21.95

The Art of Cross-Examination
Francis Wellman

QTY

I presume it is the experience of every author, after his first book is published upon an important subject, to be almost overwhelmed with a wealth of ideas and illustrations which could readily have been included in his book, and which to his own mind, at least, seem to make a second edition inevitable. Such certainly was the case with me; and when the first edition had reached its sixth impression in five months, I rejoiced to learn that it seemed to my publishers that the book had met with a sufficiently favorable reception to justify a second and considerably enlarged edition. ...

Reference   **ISBN: *1-59462-647-2***

Pages:412

MSRP $19.95

On the Duty of Civil Disobedience
Henry David Thoreau

QTY

Thoreau wrote his famous essay, On the Duty of Civil Disobedience, as a protest against an unjust but popular war and the immoral but popular institution of slave-owning. He did more than write—he declined to pay his taxes, and was hauled off to gaol in consequence. Who can say how much this refusal of his hastened the end of the war and of slavery ?

Law   **ISBN: *1-59462-747-9***

Pages:48

MSRP $7.45

Dream Psychology Psychoanalysis for Beginners
Sigmund Freud

QTY

Sigmund Freud, born Sigismund Schlomo Freud (May 6, 1856 - September 23, 1939), was a Jewish-Austrian neurologist and psychiatrist who co-founded the psychoanalytic school of psychology. Freud is best known for his theories of the unconscious mind, especially involving the mechanism of repression; his redefinition of sexual desire as mobile and directed towards a wide variety of objects; and his therapeutic techniques, especially his understanding of transference in the therapeutic relationship and the presumed value of dreams as sources of insight into unconscious desires.

Dream Psychology
Psychoanalysis for Beginners

Sigmund Freud

Psychology   **ISBN: *1-59462-905-6***

Pages:196

MSRP $15.45

The Miracle of Right Thought
Orison Swett Marden

QTY

Believe with all of your heart that you will do what you were made to do. When the mind has once formed the habit of holding cheerful, happy, prosperous pictures, it will not be easy to form the opposite habit. It does not matter how improbable or how far away this realization may see, or how dark the prospects may be, if we visualize them as best we can, as vividly as possible, hold tenaciously to them and vigorously struggle to attain them, they will gradually become actualized, realized in the life. But a desire, a longing without endeavor, a yearning abandoned or held indifferently will vanish without realization.

Self Help   **ISBN: *1-59462-644-8***

Pages:360

MSRP $25.45

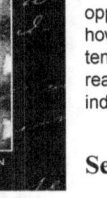

www.bookjungle.com *email: sales@bookjungle.com fax: 630-214-0564 mail: Book Jungle PO Box 2226 Champaign, IL 61825*

QTY

The Rosicrucian Cosmo-Conception Mystic Christianity *by Max Heindel*   ISBN: *1-59462-188-8*   **$38.95**
The Rosicrucian Cosmo-conception is not dogmatic, neither does it appeal to any other authority than the reason of the student. It is: not controversial, but is: sent forth in the, hope that it may help to clear...   *New Age/Religion Pages 646*

Abandonment To Divine Providence *by Jean-Pierre de Caussade*   ISBN: *1-59462-228-0*   **$25.95**
"The Rev. Jean Pierre de Caussade was one of the most remarkable spiritual writers of the Society of Jesus in France in the 18th Century. His death took place at Toulouse in 1751. His works have gone through many editions and have been republished...   *Inspirational/Religion Pages 400*

Mental Chemistry *by Charles Haanel*   ISBN: *1-59462-192-6*   **$23.95**
Mental Chemistry allows the change of material conditions by combining and appropriately utilizing the power of the mind. Much like applied chemistry creates something new and unique out of careful combinations of chemicals the mastery of mental chemistry...,   *New Age Pages 354*

The Letters of Robert Browning and Elizabeth Barret Barrett 1845-1846 vol II   ISBN: *1-59462-193-4*   **$35.95**
by Robert Browning and Elizabeth Barrett
                                                                                                              Biographies Pages 596

Gleanings In Genesis (volume I) *by Arthur W. Pink*   ISBN: *1-59462-130-6*   **$27.45**
Appropriately has Genesis been termed "the seed plot of the Bible" for in it we have, in germ form, almost all of the great doctrines which are afterwards fully developed in the books of Scripture which follow...   *Religion/Inspirational Pages 420*

The Master Key *by L. W. de Laurence*   ISBN: *1-59462-001-6*   **$30.95**
In no branch of human knowledge has there been a more lively increase of the spirit of research during the past few years than in the study of Psychology, Concentration and Mental Discipline. The requests for authentic lessons in Thought Control, Mental Discipline and...   New Age/Business Pages 422

The Lesser Key Of Solomon Goetia *by L. W. de Laurence*   ISBN: *1-59462-092-X*   **$9.95**
This translation of the first book of the "Lernegton" which is now for the first time made accessible to students of Talismanic Magic was done, after careful collation and edition, from numerous Ancient Manuscripts in Hebrew, Latin, and French...   *New Age/Occult Pages 92*

Rubaiyat Of Omar Khayyam *by Edward Fitzgerald*   ISBN:*1-59462-332-5*   **$13.95**
Edward Fitzgerald, whom the world has already learned, in spite of his own efforts to remain within the shadow of anonymity, to look upon as one of the rarest poets of the century, was born at Bredfield, in Suffolk, on the 31st of March, 1809. He was the third son of John Purcell...   Music Pages 172

Ancient Law *by Henry Maine*   ISBN: *1-59462-128-4*   **$29.95**
The chief object of the following pages is to indicate some of the earliest ideas of mankind, as they are reflected in Ancient Law, and to point out the relation of those ideas to modern thought.   *Religiom/History Pages 452*

Far-Away Stories *by William J. Locke*   ISBN: *1-59462-129-2*   **$19.45**
"Good wine needs no bush, but a collection of mixed vintages does. And this book is just such a collection. Some of the stories I do not want to remain buried for ever in the museum files of dead magazine-numbers an author's not unpardonable vanity..."   *Fiction Pages 272*

Life of David Crockett *by David Crockett*   ISBN: *1-59462-250-7*   **$27.45**
"Colonel David Crockett was one of the most remarkable men of the times in which he lived. Born in humble life, but gifted with a strong will, an indomitable courage, and unremitting perseverance...   *Biographies/New Age Pages 424*

Lip-Reading *by Edward Nitchie*   ISBN: *1-59462-206-X*   **$25.95**
Edward B. Nitchie, founder of the New York School for the Hard of Hearing, now the Nitchie School of Lip-Reading, Inc, wrote "LIP-READING Principles and Practice". The development and perfecting of this meritorious work on lip-reading was an undertaking...   *How-to Pages 400*

A Handbook of Suggestive Therapeutics, Applied Hypnotism, Psychic Science   ISBN: *1-59462-214-0*   **$24.95**
by Henry Munro
                                                                                      Health/New Age/Health/Self-help Pages 376

A Doll's House: and Two Other Plays *by Henrik Ibsen*   ISBN: *1-59462-112-8*   **$19.95**
Henrik Ibsen created this classic when in revolutionary 1848 Rome. Introducing some striking concepts in playwriting for the realist genre, this play has been studied the world over.   *Fiction/Classics/Plays 308*

The Light of Asia *by sir Edwin Arnold*   ISBN: *1-59462-204-3*   **$13.95**
In this poetic masterpiece, Edwin Arnold describes the life and teachings of Buddha. The man who was to become known as Buddha to the world was born as Prince Gautama of India but he rejected the worldly riches and abandoned the reigns of power when... Religion/History/Biographies Pages 170

The Complete Works of Guy de Maupassant *by Guy de Maupassant*   ISBN: *1-59462-157-8*   **$16.95**
"For days and days, nights and nights, I had dreamed of that first kiss which was to consecrate our engagement, and I knew not on what spot I should put my lips..."   *Fiction/Classics Pages 240*

The Art of Cross-Examination *by Francis L. Wellman*   ISBN: *1-59462-309-0*   **$26.95**
Written by a renowned trial lawyer, Wellman imparts his experience and uses case studies to explain how to use psychology to extract desired information through questioning.   *How-to/Science/Reference Pages 408*

Answered or Unanswered? *by Louisa Vaughan*   ISBN: *1-59462-248-5*   **$10.95**
Miracles of Faith in China
                                                                                                              Religion Pages 112

The Edinburgh Lectures on Mental Science (1909) *by Thomas*   ISBN: *1-59462-008-3*   **$11.95**
This book contains the substance of a course of lectures recently given by the writer in the Queen Street Hail, Edinburgh. Its purpose is to indicate the Natural Principles governing the relation between Mental Action and Material Conditions...   *New Age/Psychology Pages 148*

Ayesha *by H. Rider Haggard*   ISBN: *1-59462-301-5*   **$24.95**
Verily and indeed it is the unexpected that happens! Probably if there was one person upon the earth from whom the Editor of this, and of a certain previous history, did not expect to hear again...   *Classics Pages 380*

Ayala's Angel *by Anthony Trollope*   ISBN: *1-59462-352-X*   **$29.95**
The two girls were both pretty, but Lucy who was twenty-one who supposed to be simple and comparatively unattractive, whereas Ayala was credited, as her Bombwhat romantic name might show, with poetic charm and a taste for romance. Ayala when her father died was nineteen...   Fiction Pages 484

The American Commonwealth *by James Bryce*   ISBN: *1-59462-286-8*   **$34.45**
An interpretation of American democratic political theory. It examines political mechanics and society from the perspective of Scotsman James Bryce   *Politics Pages 572*

Stories of the Pilgrims *by Margaret P. Pumphrey*   ISBN: *1-59462-116-0*   **$17.95**
This book explores pilgrims religious oppression in England as well as their escape to Holland and eventual crossing to America on the Mayflower, and their early days in New England...   *History Pages 268*

QTY

The Fasting Cure *by Sinclair Upton*   ISBN: *1-59462-222-1* **$13.95**

In the Cosmopolitan Magazine for May, 1910, and in the Contemporary Review (London) for April, 1910, I published an article dealing with my experiences in fasting. I have written a great many magazine articles, but never one which attracted so much attention... New Age/Self Help/Health Pages 164

Hebrew Astrology *by Sepharial*   ISBN: *1-59462-308-2* **$13.45**

In these days of advanced thinking it is a matter of common observation that we have left many of the old landmarks behind and that we are now pressing forward to greater heights and to a wider horizon than that which represented the mind-content of our progenitors... Astrology Pages 144

Thought Vibration or The Law of Attraction in the Thought World   ISBN: *1-59462-127-6* **$12.95**

by William Walker Atkinson   Psychology/Religion Pages 144

Optimism *by Helen Keller*   ISBN: *1-59462-108-X* **$15.95**

Helen Keller was blind, deaf, and mute since 19 months old, yet famously learned how to overcome these handicaps, communicate with the world, and spread her lectures promoting optimism. An inspiring read for everyone... Biographies/Inspirational Pages 84

Sara Crewe *by Frances Burnett*   ISBN: *1-59462-360-0* **$9.45**

In the first place, Miss Minchin lived in London. Her home was a large, dull, tall one, in a large, dull square, where all the houses were alike, and all the sparrows were alike, and where all the door-knockers made the same heavy sound... Childrens/Classic Pages 88

The Autobiography of Benjamin Franklin *by Benjamin Franklin*   ISBN: *1-59462-135-7* **$24.95**

The Autobiography of Benjamin Franklin has probably been more extensively read than any other American historical work, and no other book of its kind has had such ups and downs of fortune. Franklin lived for many years in England, where he was agent... Biographies/History Pages 332

Name	
Email	
Telephone	
Address	
City, State ZIP	

☐ **Credit Card**   ☐ **Check / Money Order**

Credit Card Number	
Expiration Date	
Signature	

Please Mail to: Book Jungle
PO Box 2226
Champaign, IL 61825
or Fax to: 630-214-0564

ORDERING INFORMATION

web: *www.bookjungle.com*
email: *sales@bookjungle.com*
fax: *630-214-0564*
mail: *Book Jungle PO Box 2226 Champaign, IL 61825*
or PayPal *to sales@bookjungle.com*

Please contact us for bulk discounts

DIRECT-ORDER TERMS

**20% Discount if You Order
Two or More Books**
Free Domestic Shipping!
Accepted: Master Card, Visa,
Discover, American Express

www.ingramcontent.com/pod-product-compliance
Lightning Source LLC
Chambersburg PA
CBHW081159170626
46813CB00009B/3249